TWO HOURS

ALBA ARIKHA
TWO HOURS

ERIS

London • New York

Two Hours

for Gaël

We do not remember days,
we remember moments.

— Cesare Pavese

He stepped down, trying not to look long at her,
as if she were the sun, yet he saw her,
like the sun, even without looking.

—Leo Tolstoy, *Anna Karenina*

Here I am at sixteen, standing over there on the street.

Me walking towards me.

My worried eyes. My frizzy hair. My spindly legs. My rebellious tongue.

It is a freezing cold day in Manhattan, and I am getting into a taxi with my parents and my sister. We have been invited to lunch in an uptown restaurant. The sun is out, a skyscraper casts a long shadow on the pavement. I have only been in the city for a few days, and everything feels new.

The glint from the buildings.

The way the cold cuts through the air, like glass.

The ink black locks of his hair.

The violence of love.

Thirty-five years have passed, and nothing has changed. The memory has remained intact. Immutable. Burnished, like gold.

❖   ❖   ❖

In 1985, my parents announced that we were moving to Manhattan for the school term. My father, a historian, had been invited to teach at Columbia University. A friend of his, André Karlick, had offered to lend us his apartment in a luxurious doorman building on Park Avenue. A proper adventure, said our father. Unlike anything any of us had ever experienced.

I don't want a proper adventure and I'm not leaving Paris, I declared.

Neither am I, said my sister. And we don't care about Park Avenue. Or André, who never speaks to us when he sees us anyway. We don't want to go anywhere.

I shared a room with my sister in a small Parisian flat. My parents were academics. My father was French, my mother American. My bilingual upbringing revolved around books and the pursuit of all things cerebral. A world of rigour, no compromises allowed. I craved compromises, and rigour reminded me of a rapped knuckle. A knuckle rapped by the teacher who accused me of being distracted.

I don't like daydreamers, she said, as the wooden ruler came down on my eight-year-old fist. I winced but didn't cry. I seldom did in public.

André Karlick was a wealthy art dealer. He had icy blue eyes and curly hair. When my parents spoke of him it was in reverent tones. How generous and special he was. How wonderful his gallery was. How every painter he had taken on had become a household name. But I didn't care. Like my sister, I found him cold and distant, and his moneyed world did not interest me. Neither did Manhattan, especially not Park Avenue. I was not acquainted with luxury. The words 'doorman building' meant nothing to me. What is a doorman?

We're leaving in a month, my father declared, in an uncompromising tone. I have been offered an important teaching position and I must take it, whether you like it or not.

Case closed.

We argued. We often did. I shouted and stormed out of the room and retreated to my bedroom, where I wrote frantic notes of rebellion in my diary. Then I played Neil Young and listened to "Helpless", singing alone in a whisper.

Helpless.
Helpless.
Helpless.

I phoned my friend Nadine. She said that she would ask her mother whether I could come and live with them while my parents were in New York. Then I heard her mother raising her voice and saying no, no one's coming to live with us, and Nadine hung up hastily.

Later, when I was hungry, I sneaked my way into the kitchen, and there was my father, sitting at the empty table, waiting for me.

There's no point in getting angry, he said, his voice sounding softer. We can't leave you behind and this job means a lot to me. I'm sorry you feel so upset about it, but I promise you'll change your mind when we get there. New York is an exciting place. You'll be surprised.

And what if I hate it?

You have to trust me that you won't.

It's not a question of trust, I answered. You don't know my tastes. You can't predict whether I'll like it or not.

I have an idea of your tastes, my father smiled. You're my daughter, after all. New York is an exciting city and you like exciting things. Don't you?

No I don't. I hate them.

I stomped out of the kitchen. I was angry. I often was at that time. I heard my father calling me back in, but I ignored him. I went to bed on an empty stomach and cried myself to sleep. In fact, I did like exciting things. I was overdoing it with my father. This was important to him. But I couldn't help myself. Anger suffocated me, like smoke.

2

Our mother told us about André's gallery. It was on a street called West Broadway. It looked like a warehouse, with enormous bay windows and high ceilings. As far as she knew, there were no such spaces in Paris, at least not when it came to art galleries.

That's because there is no one like André Karlick, my father interjected. His eye is second to none. He knows talent when he sees it. Look at all those artists he represents. He never hesitates, never relies on other people's opinions. That's why he's so successful.

It was an important lesson in life. Not to hesitate. To trust one's instincts.

I didn't tell him that, to me, other people's opinions mattered. I wasn't sure I knew enough about myself yet. Often I felt undefined, like a blurry outline. When that happened, I found it hard to distinguish between right and wrong. I was nothing like my confident father.

In general, he added, people were ignorant. But he wasn't. He knew a lot. He hoped that, one day, I would too.

I don't think it's important to know a lot, I replied. I just want to have a nice life.

One doesn't exclude the other, my father answered.

❀   ❀   ❀

The night after our arrival there was an opening at André's gallery. My parents decided that attending it was the right thing to do, no matter the jet lag darlings.

It was very crowded, and I had never seen so many good-looking people grouped together. I felt as self-conscious as my sister did. At one point she pulled me aside: this is not a place for children, she said. We shouldn't be here. Everyone is weird.

I'm not a child, I'm a teenager, I reminded her. You're the child.

Whatever. I'm nearly a teenager too. And I still think everyone here is weird.

I agreed, but kept those thoughts to myself. Besides, there was something compelling about the atmosphere. An undeniable buzz, with lots of people staring at large canvases of skulls, billowing waves, a naked woman lying on a floating bed, another one diving into a pool. The paintings did not speak to me but clearly did to many of the people who discussed them in urgent whispers. One of the paintings being discussed was a portrait of André's wife, Lorna, a poet of some renown. She was the one diving into the pool. Lorna was very thin, with jet-black hair and hazel eyes.

Whenever her name was mentioned my father's eyes became misty. She's so beautiful, he would say, in a melancholic tone, as if her beauty were tragic.

When my mother spoke about Lorna she sounded worried. From what I gathered she was going through a difficult time. When I pressed for further details, my mother declared that it was an adult matter.

It's a complicated story. One day I'll tell you about it, she said.

Always one day. What *is* an adult matter? I was nearly an adult myself and had no time to wait. I wanted 'one day' to be today. But somehow it never was.

My sister thought that whatever was happening to Lorna had to do with André.

He looks like a wolf, she said. He eats people up.

My mother protested vehemently. The things you say... André's a good man. And he's very rich, she added, as if wealth were a personality trait. It's an honour for us to be living in his and Lorna's house, and we should all be very grateful. He's not even charging us rent!

It's not a house, it's an apartment, my father corrected her. Can't you tell the difference?

Yes, all right. An apartment which looks like a house.

3

I can see myself stepping outside that apartment building. I can see my sister too, looking small. One of the doormen is hailing us a taxi. It has begun to snow. Flakes fall around us in a thin white gloss, like Chinese paper. My father is wearing a coat which looks like a blanket. A gift from someone who lives in Spain. An expensive gift. I find it embarrassing but say nothing. I do not want to argue with my father again. And besides, this is not the moment to argue. I try to keep my teeth from chattering, which is not an easy task: I can feel the cold invading my clothes, my body. I am wearing a beige silk blouse, dark blue trousers, matching moccasins. A summer outfit, my mother had remarked earlier. You must be mad to dress that way in this weather. I have a necklace of small, coloured stars around my neck. A gift Nadine gave me as a goodbye present before my departure. The metal of the stars brushes uncomfortably against my collarbone, but I choose to ignore it. I have also chosen to ignore my mother's insistence that I wear a warmer coat. And a scarf. I would like to show off my necklace. It is a beautiful present. I love the way the stars glow. And I've never liked scarves. But the temperature in Manhattan is far colder than anything I have ever experienced. Nevertheless, I refuse to admit that my mother is right. Besides, she doesn't like scarves either.

Later, when I return home, my neck will be covered in small red spots, which will take a while to disappear. One still remains today, stark against my collarbone.

❁   ❁   ❁

André and Lorna have invited us for lunch at the Café des Artistes, a restaurant on the Upper West Side. They are staying in a hotel until the following day, when they will be boarding their plane for London.

I bet it's a fancy hotel, my sister states. With gold taps in the bathrooms and stuff.

They live a fancy life, my mother declares. They can afford it.

That's nice, my sister says, her eyes looking dreamy.

Not really, I reply. I think fancy lives are boring.

Fine, says my mother. Well, fancy or not, we'll be having lunch with them, and they'll be bringing their son, Alexander. He's sixteen, like you. Lorna tells me you were born a few days apart.

I don't tell her that, as a rule, I never like other people's children.

4

A man with white gloves opens the door and asks us to follow him into a room covered with murals. The Café des Artistes is an expensive restaurant; I can see that right away. The men wear suits and most of the women are carefully made up with coiffed hair. André and Lorna have arrived before us and greet us warmly. Lorna is wearing a white crocheted dress. She doesn't look like the other women. Knee-high boots emphasise her long, slim legs. Dangly earrings, shaped like feathers, hang from her ears. I don't think they suit her. But she's undeniably beautiful.

Alexander, this is Clara, she says, pushing her son gently towards me.

Yeah, he answers gruffly.

His black curly hair covers half his face. All I can make out is a pointy chin and thick lips. I decide immediately that I don't like him.

Our table is facing one of the many murals covering the walls. This one, in earth-tone colours, depicts naked nymphs frolicking in sylvan glades. I look at their breasts and then catch Alexander's eye studying them too. I blush and force myself to yawn.

The tablecloth and napkins are made of thick white cotton. The wine glasses shine and the waiters hover over us in expectation. A couple at the next table are holding hands above their plates, as if they're attending a seance. The woman wears a heavy necklace with a huge stone that sparkles. The man smiles at her. He wears a pink shirt and his hair looks wet. When the couple speak to each other, their voices are so hushed that I wonder how they can even hear each other. I am not used to such restaurants, to such people, and I feel out of place.

Alexander is seated next to me, and he doesn't speak at all. He also looks out of place, although perhaps not for the same reasons I do. He has pushed his black locks back. He is very good-looking: I can see that now. He has dark green eyes and looks remarkably like his mother. When his gaze momentarily settles on mine, I feel something akin to what I have read about in books. A flutter of the heart. I have never experienced anything like it before. I had a boyfriend once, when I was fifteen. He was handsome and gregarious, but we had little in common. He had a passion for horses and spoke of little else. Nevertheless, we spent a lot of time kissing and groping each other in his apartment when his parents were out. Then, after a couple of weeks, we broke up. What upset me most was the fact that I had failed to fall in love with him. That he had left me for another girl seemed immaterial. I wanted to know what love felt like. Looked like. Tasted like. I wonder if Alexander has ever experienced it. Or if he feels the same flutter as I do. If so, he doesn't give it away. He doesn't give anything away. He spends most of the meal ignoring me. Or perhaps he is bored. I could take it personally, but I don't; I find him tantalisingly mysterious.

Just before dessert is served, he speaks to me. His voice lies somewhere between boy and man. It sounds cracked, as though it might shatter. This makes my heart flutter even faster. Alexander asks me what it's like to live in Paris.

It's normal, I answer.

I take where I live for granted. I have never given it much thought, unlike school, which takes up most of my time.

I wish school didn't exist, I say. Except for my friends. I like them.

I don't have many friends, he admits.

I don't either.

But you just said you did...

I guess I care about some of my friends. And reading, I add quickly. I like to read.

Alexander's face lights up. He asks me who my favourite authors are.

I start listing them, and our preferences slide into each other in perfect harmony: I can see from the look in his eyes that he's impressed. But Alexander's reading list is far more extensive and sophisticated than mine—as is his way of expressing himself. I've never met a sixteen-year-old like him. He mentions authors I've never heard of, others whom I have. He speaks quickly and passionately:

I find Dostoevsky's exploration of the morality of radicalism fascinating, he says. I think that Raskolnikov has got to be one of the most complex, innovative characters in modern literature.

I don't know about categories of literature, or the morality of radicalism. I haven't read Dostoevsky. The name conjures up something fiery. A warrior. Dostoevsky warrior. Alexander warrior.

But I cannot admit my ignorance. I must find a way of shifting the conversation. What about Jane Austen? I venture timidly.

I've just read *Pride and Prejudice* at school, in French: *Orgueil et préjugés*. I admire Elizabeth Bennett. I loved the book.

But Alexander did not: Jane Austen is too concerned with money and marriage, he declares. I prefer Henry James. I think he was more intelligent and sensitive. And he wrote about nineteenth-century family dynamics in a more interesting way.

Did he? I cannot comment because I've never read Henry James, or given much thought to nineteenth-century family dynamics: I clearly have lots of catching up to do.

And anyway, I don't like reading about England, Alexander mumbles.

Why not?

Because I don't like it. I don't want to move there. I hate moving. I hate London.

But you've never been! I didn't want to move to New York, but in the end it's been OK.

He shrugs his shoulders. You were lucky. And

London is not the same as New York. I'm sure I'll hate it. In general, I hate everything.

I've never met anyone who hated everything.

But you just said that you love all these books!

Yes. But literature isn't life. Things don't always resolve themselves in life, but they do in books. That's why I like them better.

That's so true, I gush, then wish I could undo the gushing.

And my parents don't understand me, he continues.

I feel the same about my parents. They don't understand me either.

Yeah, I concur, trying to sound American.

And they don't know, he adds.

What?

That they're making a mistake and that we should stay here. That we shouldn't go to London. I hate places I don't know.

But maybe if you get to know it you won't hate it anymore...

Alexander looks at me: I suppose. But it's a mistake, he repeats. We shouldn't go to London.

I quickly tell him that I often feel the same as he does about travelling to unknown places, although that is not technically true. I have an insatiable curiosity about other continents, specifically South America. Nadine and I have decided that one day we will learn Spanish and live in Guatemala together.

But I hold that information back.

A waiter wheels in some desserts on a trolley. André smiles at me for the first time. Help yourself, he says. Have whatever you'd like. You're my guests.

He motions towards the trolley, with its array of cakes, mousses, and tarts. There is something about the ease of André's gesture, about the way he can just say *help yourself*, which makes me aware of the divide between him and my family. In general, I cannot help myself to whatever I'd like. Neither can my parents. And we always seem to be other people's guests.

I wonder what it might feel like to have money and power. Then I look at Alexander and decide that it is probably not a good thing. His parents might be rich, but they misunderstand him. I don't. I understand everything about him. I've never met anyone like Alexander Karlick. I find him utterly compelling. Entrancing. Beautiful.

5

Alexander Karlick.

6

Just like my father said, André and Lorna Karlick's apartment is spacious and luxurious, about three times the size of our Parisian rental.

Because they're planning on renovating it when they return, a lot of the furniture has been removed and replaced by functional pieces, apart from in the sitting room, which I've been told remains as it was. It is filled with beautiful antique pieces and oriental rugs. There are fragile objects displayed on shelves, just like in a museum. A grand piano sits in the corner of the room, looking untouched. My mother has mentioned that Lorna used to play very well, then gave it up, but that André lives in the hope that she might take it up again. Something tells me that he might be hoping in vain. That Lorna will never take it up again. But perhaps I am judging her. How well do I know her, after all? Sometimes I do that. I tend to judge people hastily. I feel foolish when I turn out to be wrong. Naïve. I wonder if I'm wrong about Lorna. I wonder if Alexander judges people too. Chances are he does, but in a different way. A wiser way. I wish I could see him again. Ask him more about his family, and why it is his mother will no longer play the piano. I hope that London will turn out well for him. That he will make some friends there. Perhaps I could send him a postcard? Or perhaps not.

In the meantime, I spend my first night in his Manhattan bedroom, which has been stripped of all its belongings. I had hoped for a few clues to his personality but find little. The desk has been emptied, as has his closet. It is a plain, nondescript space with a bed, a desk, and, on the wall, a large map of the world. There are few books left: an Oxford dictionary, a bound edition of *The Iliad*, collected poems by a woman called Anna Akhmatova, and a large volume entitled *How to Become a Stamp Collector*. I try to feel Alexander's presence in the room, but little remains, apart from a note I find, presumably in his handwriting, in the wastepaper basket under his desk. *Musil. Ask S about Maine.* I spend an inordinate amount of time trying to decipher who Musil and S are, until I finally fall asleep.

7

The next morning is a Sunday. We are all sitting in pyjamas, drinking orange juice from the biggest carton I have ever seen, and eating our first bagels with cream cheese. People here like to eat these on weekends, our mother has explained. Sometimes with smoked salmon too.

Yum, says my sister.

Did you use to have them when you were our age? I ask.

My mother shakes her head. No, we didn't. I don't think we even knew about them.

My sister declares it's the best thing she's ever eaten. She asks my mother if one is allowed to eat bagels during the week too. My father answers. Why not? I don't see why that should be a problem. Compared to France, this country has very few problems, he says, as he pours himself a cup of tea. And if it does, eating bagels during the week is not one of them. He smiles at both of us broadly—ever since we've arrived, he's been in a particularly good mood.

The phone rings. When she picks it up, right outside the kitchen door, I can hear my mother speaking in a demure voice, as if she doesn't know the person well. She comes back in to say that André was just on the phone. His son Alexander will be coming by in about thirty minutes to pick up a book he needs for London.

As soon as I hear these words I spit my bagel out onto my plate. Thirty minutes? I cannot, under any circumstances, let Alexander Karlick see me in my pyjamas.

You're so gross! my sister shouts. What's the matter with you?

Shut up you worm, I retort, before rushing off to the bathroom.

I jump into the shower, brush my hair, apply some makeup and a dash of perfume, and fret about what to wear. A dress? A skirt? Trousers? Yes. No. Yes: I decide on a short skirt, a white shirt, and black ballerinas I bought before leaving. I've managed to get ready in the space of fifteen minutes: it is a first. My mother enters, holding some sheets in her hand. You look nice, she says. And the room looks nice too, she notices—I've made the bed, which is unlike me. Where are you going?

I'm not going anywhere, I just don't like boys seeing me in my pyjamas, I reply tartly.

My mother smiles, and I understand that she knows. This is not about boys in general but one in particular. I feel my cheeks turn red and I avoid her gaze. I cannot think of anything more embarrassing than my family being privy to my secret crushes. But this is not the time to quibble about such matters. Alexander is about to arrive, and nothing is more important than that.

A buzzer rings from downstairs. My father says it's probably the doorman. But where is the intercom? All of us go in frantic search of it while the buzzing becomes more insistent until it stops—as does my heart. Because this means that Alexander will not be coming after all: we didn't know where the intercom was, and the doorman probably assumed that we were out. I will never see Alexander again. I feel tears well up and run to my room to hide them. Which is when the doorbell rings.

Alexander! I hear my mother exclaim. How nice to see you!

I take a deep breath, dab my eyes quickly. I hear his footsteps approaching and suddenly there he is, standing in front of me.

Hi, he says.

His hair is covering his face again, but this time I know what lies beneath. He is wearing jeans and a black Fruit of the Loom T-shirt, and he is carrying a small backpack. He looks older than sixteen. Taller than I remembered.

We walk into his bedroom together. He looks at the quasi-bare shelf and pulls down the *Iliad*. It's one of my favourites, he tells me. I couldn't go to London without it, he adds, placing it inside his backpack.

I smile and mutter something nonsensical. What is there to say? I know that he is lying. Not about the *Iliad*, which probably is one of his favourites. But about the fact that he did not stop by to collect a book but to see me again. I know it because I can read it in his eyes. I can read it in the way both of us stand awkwardly close to each other, nearly touching but not. I can read it in the way we speak to each other, our seemingly anodyne conversation concealing layers of youthful lust and desire. I can hear it in the way he says, it was really nice to meet you Clara, and the way he pronounces my name. As clear as spring water. I can feel the high voltage current between us, so high it might combust. Now he reaches out his hand towards mine and the tips of our fingers touch, then interlace. His palm burns. He moves closer and pulls the hair away from his face. His lips reach slowly towards mine. Which is when my sister chooses to barge in.

Just as he is about to kiss me.

Have you seen my black pen? she asks, as Alexander steps back, just in time.

No, I haven't, I declare, in a surprisingly composed voice. In fact, I would kill her if I could. We're busy talking here, can't you see?

Yeah whatever, she replies, before walking away.

Alexander clears his throat. I should go anyway. Our plane is leaving soon.

Yes of course.

We make our way to the front door. Please say goodbye to your parents for me, he says.

I will.

We look at each other again. I swallow hard. He presses the button for the elevator. Maybe we could, like, write to each other, he ventures, turning one last time to face me.

That sounds nice, I answer, as the elevator arrives. The doorman holds the door open for Alexander. Hello Master Karlick, he says. Alexander steps inside and gives me a small wave.

And then he is gone.

8

9

In my bedroom I inhabit the sliver of space he left behind. The force of him. The smell of him. I stand where he stood. The feel of his gravity beneath me. His burning palm against mine. His green gaze.

At night my tears cover the pillowcase. It is still damp in the morning.

10

Of the books in Alexander's bookshelf, the one that intrigues me most is the volume of Anna Akhmatova's poetry. I had read about her in the introduction to the well-worn book. Her talent, her beauty, her life. If Alexander admires this woman, then so must I. And I do. I am gripped by what I read. I love him all the more for loving her. Then, on p. 76, I find these words underlined: *Tell me how you kiss.* The poem is called "The Guest" and he has underlined those words, because they are directed at me. There is no doubt in my mind. Our brutally interrupted kiss is proof that I am right. Alexander must have underlined it quickly when I had my back turned. Then again, did I have my back turned at all? We seemed to be facing each other the whole time. I decide that the logistics are irrelevant here. What matters is the evidence:

> He lifted his thin hand
> and lightly stroked the flowers:
> "Tell me how men kiss you,
> <u>tell me how you kiss</u>."

By the end of that week, I know everything there is to know about Anna Akhmatova. I discuss her with my parents, who appear impressed.

We didn't realise you were interested in Russian poets, my father says. How did that happen?

It just happened. There's a lot about me you don't know, I retort.

11

In the evening I picture Alexander sitting at his desk, going through his stamp collection with his magnifying glass. Sometimes he stops and recites a few Akhmatova poems to me. He recites from "The Guest" then kisses me in between words. Tell (kiss) me (kiss) how (kiss) you (kiss) kiss (kiss).

Then he returns to his new discovery, a 1974 Burundi stamp, illustrated with a black and yellow butterfly, which may or may not be worth a fortune.

Meanwhile my sister, far from African butterflies and Alexander's kisses, sleeps in what is euphemistically called the maid's room, a space no bigger than a closet, which barely accommodates a small bed and a side table. She is not happy there.

You must take turns in the small room, the two of you, my mother declares. You must be fair to your sister.

I will not be fair to my sister, who is responsible for interrupting what could have been one of the most beautiful moments in my life: she barged into my room just as I was about to kiss Alexander. Because of her, he stopped. For that she must pay—and for a long time. I succeed in making sure she remains in the maid's closet. What's the point of moving all our stuff back and forth? It's too complicated, I tell my mother.

My sister puts up a fight, then eventually gives up. I like it when I win.

Even though I only ever seem to win at home.

12

The imposing 88th Street Beaux-Arts building we live in is tended by doormen who all wear the same uniform: a black double-breasted jacket with shiny gold buttons, matching trousers with gold piping, and a black, gold-rimmed cap.

The uniforms swallow up their faces and I find it hard to distinguish one man from the next. I suspect that if I were to see them in regular clothing, I probably wouldn't recognise them at all. But they would recognise me. The Frenchie sisters, they call us.

I like that.

Hey yo' Frenchie sisters how ya doin', is the way Pedro, the elevator man, usually greets us. He proceeds to wish us a happy day at school. I rarely hear him say anything else, except for the occasional comment about the weather.

The school in question is the French lycée on 93rd Street.

My sister and I take a crosstown bus together every morning.

I enjoy my new friends, although I don't like some of the stricter teachers. When I tell my father he brushes it aside.

You are lucky girls, he says. And we're only here for six months. No complaining allowed.

And I do feel lucky; we all do. My father was right. This is a good place to be. And I have never seen him in a better mood than he is in Manhattan. It's easier to be a Jew here, he once mentions in passing.

I'm surprised because I hadn't realised that being a Jew could still be difficult.

Most of the time I don't give religion a second thought. We celebrate Christmas and light candles for Hanukkah. I would be a Buddhist if I could, my father often says. I can't stand religion.

My mother disagrees quietly. Everything about her is quiet.

But perhaps that's because everything about my father is so loud.

13

Our mother loved another boy once. His name was Haim Goshem.

She met him at the age of seventeen, in a local library in Brooklyn, where she lived. She described him as rake thin, with broad ears and large hands which moved around a lot. He came from a relatively wealthy and educated family: our mother did not. And she knew that her parents would not approve of Haim. He wasn't devout, like her family was. As far as they were concerned, their daughter's future was to lie within devout boundaries.

The two of them met in secret. Haim had a much larger grasp of the world than our mother had, and it made her aware of the narrowness of her upbringing. He read books, he recited poetry, he listened to music she didn't even know existed. One afternoon Haim took her to his apartment. School had ended unexpectedly early. It was the first secular apartment she had ever visited, as she described it. A few streets away, a universe apart. It had books, and posters on the walls, and music playing on a gramophone. It had everything she didn't have, including parents who were scientists. Did her parents even know what science was?

Eventually she told them about Haim Goshem. That he was the boy she loved and wanted to marry.

Her mother answered that marriage wasn't about love, and her father said that her future husband Itzhak (our mother couldn't remember his surname) had already been selected for her. A good boy from a good family, *baruch hashem*.

But I want to choose my own husband! our mother cried out. I don't want to marry Itzhak! I want to marry the man I love!

You must listen to us, her parents said. You don't know what's best for you. And we do. You must trust us.

She pretended to trust them. But behind her parents' backs she continued to meet Haim in secret. We'll run away and get married when you turn eighteen, he promised her.

But when she turned eighteen Haim admitted that he didn't want to get married after all. He had spoken to his parents, and they had agreed that it was important he finish his studies first. And she was religious, which made things more complicated. He didn't want to lead a religious life.

Neither do I! our mother assured him.

But Haim had made up his mind. It will be easier if we say goodbye. Good luck with everything, were his last words.

Our mother was devastated. So devastated she decided to leave home. She packed her bags for Manhattan, where she met our father. Together they moved to Paris. By then, her parents had given up on interfering in her life. They realised that they could no longer control their daughter. In meeting Haim Goshem, our mother had understood that the freedom she sought was an essential component of her identity. She trusted her parents, but she wasn't like them. She had never been and never would be.

So they gave her their blessing and sent her on her way.

My sister and I quizzed her endlessly about that story.

Did you love Haim more than our father?

Absolutely not. If anything, I loved your father more. I was more mature by the time I met him. In retrospect, it is quite clear that Haim Goshem was not the right man for me.

Whatever happened to the Itzhak you were meant to marry?

No idea. I assume he must have married someone else.

But if you had married Haim Goshem, then we daughters wouldn't have existed!

That's correct.

But maybe other daughters would have existed instead? And a son too?

Yes. Possibly a son too.

Would you have preferred a son?

Of course not! I love my girls.

And did you ever see or speak to Haim Goshem again?

No, and that was fine by me. I wanted nothing more to do with Haim Goshem, who by the way went on to become a famous philosopher. But I never cared much for philosophy anyway.

14

Our mother took us to visit her parents when we were younger. My grandfather, a strict and distant man, owned a corner shop in Brooklyn. My grandmother manned the till. She wore a blue kerchief and smiled a lot. Her dress looked like a nightgown and her cheeks were warm when I kissed them. She was very happy to see us—our mother rarely visited. When she announced we couldn't stay very long, she cried a little, and my mother hugged her. Not the way she hugged me or my sister, but as if this was a task she wanted to get out of the way. As if she felt awkward demonstrating any sort of love towards her own mother.

Right before we left, our grandfather gave us sweets he kept in a special tin for the neighbourhood children. That is all I remember of him. A tall, slightly stooped man with a lazy eye, who handed us sweets in gold wrappers. Here, here, he said. Then he patted our heads with his long fingers.

My grandfather died shortly after our visit, followed by our grandmother a few months later.

Her heart gave out one morning, said my mother. She had just returned home with the shopping when she collapsed. A neighbour found her on the ground, still clutching her shopping bags, a broken jar of pickles at her feet.

I don't remember my mother mourning hers. I don't remember her crying, either. She was seldom mentioned afterwards, and eventually I forgot what she had looked like. But impressions remained. The blue kerchief on her head. The warmth of her cheeks. The jar of broken pickles at her feet. The way my mother had hugged her, and the look of discomfort on her face.

15

These are happy months. I tell my parents that I'd like to stay in New York for good. I don't admit that one of the reasons is that I want to see Alexander again and live in the same city as he does. I've received a postcard from him. On the back is a reproduction of a Jackson Pollock painting. His handwriting is tidy, with a quasi-feminine elegance to it.

Dear Clara,

London is fine. Not great but fine. It rains a lot. We live in a house with a garden. It's different. School reminds me of my New York school but better. Do you know Jackson Pollock? I think abstract expressionism is the answer to everything. How are you liking NYC? There's a coffee shop on Lexington and 70th which does great breakfasts. You should go there. I'm reading Graham Greene and I love him. I think you will too. It would be nice to see you again when I get back. I think it will be this summer.

Alexander.

The card sends me into paroxysms of delight, and I sleep with it under my pillow before its nocturnal creases convince me to stash it away somewhere safer.

I investigate abstract expressionism, Jackson Pollock in particular. But it doesn't seem to me to be the answer to everything. Is there such a thing anyway? The problem with the world as I see it is that it doesn't seem to come down to one answer only. Nevertheless, I feel a strong connection with Clyfford Still, rather than Pollock, and tell Alexander so. The splash of yellow amidst the blue. A rebel yellow. It feels good to disagree with him. To discuss pictorial rebels with him, among other subjects. He isn't there with me— but I pretend that he is. In his bedroom I hold many imaginary conversations with Alexander and, to my relief, I win the arguments every time.

And then there is the matter of the coffee shop. I drag my bewildered parents to 70th Street, insisting we must eat there from then on. Apart from a few breakfasts, which they seem to enjoy, my father deems the food inedible. Whoever told you to come to such a place? he grumbles. They're very nice people, but I'm not eating here again.

For once, I do not know what to reply. In fact,

Alexander had only mentioned breakfast. So I say nothing and end up going there alone. It feels grown-up to do so. And I always carry a book with me: I have bought myself every Graham Greene novel I could find—there are many. I devour them all and pick *Our Man in Havana* as my favourite. I write to Alexander about it but do not hear back from him. Although I am mildly disappointed, I do not worry unduly. I am confident I will see him again. And that confidence guides me forward. He is waiting to see me again, just as I am waiting to see him. I thrive in New York, especially academically. My parents take note. I plead for them to stay for longer than a year. But my mother explains that it is impossible. I'd love to stay longer too, she admits. And so would your father. But he has commitments.

His work. His books. His teaching. His wellbeing.

My mother works too, as a translator, but somehow my father is the one who always matters more.

16

In the spring, three months after we have arrived, Lorna suddenly dies, in London. We are not told why, just that we have to move out immediately. I am in shock. We all are. I've never known anyone who has died before, apart from my grandparents, who were old and ill.

Death to me is for old, ill people, not thin and beautiful poets like Lorna.

I feel that there is more to the story and ask my parents to elaborate. They answer evasively: she died, and that is tragic enough.

I don't tell them that I had a feeling about her. I couldn't describe what it was, only that it hid inside me, like a half-formed whisper.

I attend the funeral. Everyone is crying. Alexander is there, dressed in black.

I see him from afar, then closer. His skin is parched and red.

He has been crying. He is still crying. The broken, green sorrow of his eyes briefly settles on mine. Then he turns his back on me, like a wall. It is as if he didn't want to see me. Or didn't want me to see him. I would like to touch him, to comfort him, to hold him against me, but all I get is the wall.

It is an image that will remain permanently ingrained in my mind.

17

We move into Columbia University accommodation. The flat is on Riverside Drive and 112th Street. A drab and sad apartment. But it doesn't matter as much as what happened to Lorna. I now know how Alexander's mother died, because I saw it in the newspaper. My parents tried to hide it from me but I saw it: the Karlick gallery is very well known, as is its owner. Lorna killed herself.

Jumped off the balcony of their London hotel room.

Suicide. It sounds like the searing slit of a knife.

Later, more information comes out. Lorna had something called depression.

And there is more: she was born in Auschwitz. I know about Auschwitz; we often talk about it at home: the Holocaust. The persecutions of the Jews. How some members of my mother's family died a terrible death.

Antisemitism is history's oldest hatred, my father tells us. Still alive and well today. It's unlikely to ever disappear.

We also learned about the Holocaust at school. The death machine. The way the camps were liberated. The Nuremberg trials. But somehow, despite my blood line and my father's words, it feels distant to me. Being Jewish to my parents is important in theory, but not in practice. I know little about my religion and have never felt the need to explore it. But the notion that anyone could have been given life in an extermination camp staggers me. Lorna was born in 1945, two weeks before the Soviets liberated the camp. Her mother succumbed to typhus one month later. She never got to know her daughter.

Her beautiful, fragile daughter.

I don't think she was able to live with her history, my father tells us.

This is the only comment he will ever make in relation to Lorna's death.

She wasn't able to live with her history

18

I try to get in touch with Alexander. I ring him once, with trembling fingers. A woman, presumably a maid, answers the phone. She tells me that Alexander doesn't live in the building anymore, but she will ask him to call me when she sees him next time. I don't ask her where he is or when next time will be. A void has opened below my feet. A void of sorrow and longing. I wish I could comfort Alexander. Kiss him. Touch him. The way his lips moved towards mine.

Tell me how you kiss.

19

I have changed, but Paris hasn't: it never does.

New York seems to be constantly moving, but Paris is still in comparison. Beautiful and still. Still and sad. Like Alexander. My first love. The most exciting person I have ever met. The most brilliant, heart-breaking, beautiful person I have ever met. I wish I could have consoled him. I wish I could have told him that I now understand why he hated the idea of going to London.

It was as if he knew all along.

It makes me love him even more.

20

A month after Lorna's death we move again, to Berlin this time. My father has been asked to teach at the Humboldt University for six months. A very prestigious position, our mother explains. That is why we're cutting our New York stay short. School is nearly over anyway. Also, after everything that happened with the Karlicks the city has lost its shine. It's all too tragic to stay here, she says.

Not for me it isn't. I don't care about prestige. I don't want to go to Berlin. New York has not lost its shine, because Alexander is there. He is the shine. Except that he has vanished, and I don't know how to find him.

21

In Berlin I attend another French lycée and struggle, as does my sister.

In the evenings, after I've finished my homework, I write letters to Alexander. Long ones which I will never send. I kiss the letters of his name and cry for him in the dark. I reread, over and over, his postcard with the Jackson Pollock painting. I caress the tips of his jet-blue words with my fingers.

I found those letters, and his postcard, years later. I was emptying my old closet in Paris and there they were: tear-stained letters on bright yellow paper, lying inside a forgotten shoebox. The dog-eared corners of the postcard were worse than I remembered them. But his handwriting was as clear as day.

22

We leave Berlin shortly after Christmas. I return to Paris with my mother and sister, while my father stays on.

I will come and visit as often as I can, he promises.

He visits, but there is something different about him.

I'm not sure what it is, but I know that it is serious because my father looks preoccupied, and I catch my mother crying.

I've rarely seen her cry before, and it worries me. I plead for her to tell me what's wrong. I'm nearly seventeen, I say, I understand things.

She looks at me and smiles through her tears. It's a grown-up problem, is all she volunteers.

The grown-up problem is a woman in Berlin. Her name is Brigitte and she has blonde hair. She has been having an affair with my father. I only know this because I overheard my mother telling a friend on the phone.

I wait for her to confess, but she doesn't. And I do not dare bring it up. I am aware of the heaviness of the subject.

Heavy like Lorna's death.

Our parents avoid heavy subjects as if they might become contaminated by them.

23

Our father returns to Paris and everything is normal again, as if nothing had happened. As if blonde Brigitte from Berlin had never come between him and our mother. As if their marriage hadn't nearly broken down.

Like many occurrences in my family life, this is one I must contemplate alone.

And when I confront my mother about it years later, after Katia's birth, she tells me that I imagined the whole thing. That I must have misheard whatever it was she said that day on the phone. There never was a blonde woman from Berlin called Brigitte. There never was an affair. Your father would never have done such a thing, she adds defensively.

I did little and luck came to me, my father reminds me often. You must do the same. You must wait for it to happen.

Something tells me that he is wrong. That if I wait it will never happen. Luck is what matters most—but it only happens at intervals. Therefore, I must be prepared for that interval. Just like Seneca said. *Luck is what happens when preparation meets opportunity.*

Then again, opportunity is a concept I haven't quite grasped, a grown-up concept. I am still young. The future is an opaque window. I cannot see through its pane. Not yet. But I hope that, when I do, the view will be clear. Unobstructed.

25

I study *Oedipus Rex* at school. I read how, after he had received the prophecy that his infant son would one day murder him and marry his mother, Laius, the King of Thebes, gave orders that the baby be left to die in the mountains. Once the rescued, and now adult, Oedipus found out about the prophecy, he fled to escape his fate—only to find himself unwittingly fulfilling it. What does this mean? That all prophecies are self-fulfilling?

Until I met Alexander, I believed that my future would be determined by free will and nothing else. No powers of fate or other external forces.

But now I believe in coincidences and connections.

If my mother had married Haim Goshem I wouldn't be here today, writing this story.

If she hadn't left for Manhattan, she might never have met my father—and I wouldn't be here today either.

If Lorna hadn't survived Auschwitz, Alexander wouldn't have existed.

If we hadn't moved to New York, I wouldn't have met Alexander.

If I hadn't met Alexander, I wouldn't have become the woman I am on the way to becoming.

If Lorna hadn't died, I might have stayed longer in New York.

I might have become Alexander's girlfriend and possibly his wife.

My parents probably wouldn't have gone to Berlin.

If they hadn't gone to Berlin, my father wouldn't have had the affair with Brigitte.

If he hadn't had the affair with Brigitte, my parents would be happier.

If they were happier, I wouldn't be so angry.

Or perhaps the unhappy one is me.

The fights at home have become untenable. My father is strict and uncompromising. I answer back. I scream, cry, slam doors. The neighbours complain about the noise. I am thrown out of school for unruly behaviour. My grades are poor, but I don't care. My companions are books and films: we understand each other. When I'm not reading a book, I'm watching a film. Somehow I manage to watch up to three or four a week, alone or with friends. I skip school and jump on a bus. I enjoy these small acts of truancy. Will I ever get caught? Even if I am, it will not matter. Films are an education in themselves. Especially the ones I like to see, Hollywood films noirs and anything French or Italian. I get off at the St Michel-St Germain stop and walk quickly towards one of the old cinemas that line the streets of St Germain-des-Prés or those closer to the Sorbonne. They attract a faithful clientele which often queues round the corner to secure a seat. The French love old films and I'm no exception.

I ensconce myself in my seat, usually in the back row, even if the room is empty. I wait, with bated breath, for the curtain to open.

I love it when the lights go out, the screen crackles, and the titles appear. The moment of communion between the screen and me.

The faces. The plot. The dialogue. This is where I belong. Inside a book. Or a film. The perfect overlapping of worlds. Simone de Beauvoir said that *what matters is to be fascinated by a singular world that overlaps with mine and yet is other.* I will plunge into that singular world. I will overlap and become other: a character in a Godard film. I will take a lover and live on a barge somewhere in Bourgogne. His name is Vincent. I'm nearly seventeen and still a virgin, but that won't last. We will read books and recite poetry to each other and smoke cigarettes. I love cigarettes. I will wear miniskirts with stiletto shoes. I will apply a thick black kohl line to my eyelids, like Brigitte Bardot in the movie *Contempt.* At night, my lover and I will eat dinner in small Bourguignon restaurants with white tablecloths and French folk songs being played in the background. We will hold hands across the table and gaze into each other's eyes. Then we will go home and Vincent will make love to me.

He will smell of smoke and night air.

26

I see a short film by the director Claude Chabrol, *La Muette.*

The mute one. A young Parisian boy is traumatised by his parents' constant bickering. As a result, he steals his mother's earplugs and shuts himself off from his surroundings.

He now lives in his own parallel world. One day his mother falls down the stairs and screams for help. With his earplugs in, the son hears nothing. His mother lies in a pool of blood, at the bottom of the stairs. In the last scene, the young boy can be seen roaming the streets of Paris in a state of shock. I am also in a state of shock. So much so that, when I get home, I find myself crying uncontrollably in my bedroom. It isn't only the woman's screams which pierce my heart. It is the young boy's pain and the aftermath of his decision. I relate to him and yet I hate him. By enclosing himself inside his own wall of silence, he has failed to save the person he loved the most.

It is an intolerable thought.

Later, as I'm about to fall asleep, I realise what it is about the film.

The boy reminds me of Alexander. Alexander and his mother. I think of him every day, and I shiver with longing every time I do. Cold longing.

I think of Lorna and how she threw herself out of a hotel window. The image haunts me. Did she know, before she got dressed that morning, that she would kill herself? What did she wear? What was she feeling and why did she do it? Did she not think of her son?

I have heard that André has met a new woman and moved in with her.

That Alexander has been sent to a boarding school somewhere in Connecticut. That is where he was when I called him. It seems a harsh sentence. Where I come from, no one goes to boarding school unless they've done something wicked.

Perhaps Alexander has done something wicked. Or perhaps his father felt that life would be easier without his downcast son around. I never sensed that father and son got along. I wonder if Alexander still hates everything around him. I wonder how often he thinks of his mother. Probably very often, I surmise. I think of her too. I repeatedly ask my parents about Lorna. I would like to know. Why. How. Why?

But like many other painful events in my family's life, this is not one they feel comfortable talking about. We don't know, they answer. No one knows why these things happen.

So just like Alexander and the boy in the film, I retreat behind my own wall of silence.

27

I am sent to an American boarding school. A rich relative foots the bill. I now have something in common with Alexander. Wicked me, wicked Alexander. I wish I could tell him. Find him and tell him. But I wouldn't know where to start looking. My parents are no longer in touch with André, for reasons unknown to me.

The school is in the Vermont countryside, and I decide to hate it. It would have been acceptable had it been in New York. But Vermont? I have never liked the countryside. I only like cities, like Alexander does. Pavements. Cafés. Bookshops. Bakeries. There will be none of that there. Only endless green, rural spaces. Therefore, it is easier to hate than to love. Alexander was right. I can see it now. Alexander everywhere. Hatred requires less effort and makes for a quicker exit. But in this case there is no exit to be made.

My father is unmoved. One year, he says. Had you not been so rebellious this wouldn't have happened. I must get through it and be strong. One year.

28

I attempt to befriend my classmates, but soon decide that it isn't worth the effort. I cannot relate to them. What's the point? I have a strong French accent, I don't particularly enjoy outdoor activities, which are part of the school ethic, and my family is not rich, unlike most of the students there. As a result, none of them approaches me. Or perhaps they do, but I don't give their fumbling efforts a chance until the very end, at which point I realise I have made a mistake. These are intelligent students, some of them inordinately so. But it is too late to backtrack. The only people who seem to express any interest in me are the teachers. They are kind, enquire if I'm settling in well, if there's anything they can do to help.

No, nothing, thank you, I repeatedly tell them. Nothing at all.

At Thanksgiving, the history teacher invites me to his family home. You must join us, he insists. The lunch, served at 4.00 p.m. is a long-winded affair. But

I enjoy myself: the food, the conversation. His wife, a woman from Bangladesh with a beautiful smile, asks me lots of questions about Paris. She dreams of going there, she says. Someone gets up to play the piano then breaks into song. The crowd joins in. I don't know the songs, mostly jazz numbers, but I like the music. I feel relaxed, momentarily happy. I wish I could live with my history teacher's family, rather than in the cold room at school. Because it is cold in Vermont. A bone-chilling cold, which only intensifies in the dark months. One Friday evening the English teacher, a bearded man with wide eyes, reads out an Ernest Hemingway short story. A gripping one. The students listen to him intently, as do I, drinking cider from paper cups. The teacher's voice is deep and resonant. A fire blazes in the hearth. I can see snow falling outside. There is every reason for me to enjoy this, but I decide not to. I return to my room midway through the story, feeling sorry for myself. My roommate, a redhead from Arkansas who avoids me when she can, is out with her boyfriend. I am alone. Stubborn, French, sad, and alone. I wish I had not left before the end of the story, but if I go back in there now it will make me look like a fool. I cannot look like a fool. So I stay in my room and cry myself to sleep.

The next day there is a snowstorm. The snow is so thick I can barely see out of the window. And my throat hurts. I stay in bed and reread letters I have received from various friends, filling me in on the latest gossip. The history teacher is a sadist. There is a new café they all go to now, by the old Halles market. A new film has come out: *Betty Blue*, with Jean-Hugues Anglade. My friends fancy him. Sophie thinks she spotted him at the Palace night club the other evening. He was having a drink with a supermodel who could have been Cindy Crawford. Although she spoke French, so she wasn't sure. Did Cindy Crawford speak French? And when was I planning on returning to Paris?

Then a letter from home. My sister tells me about school, the new cat, and how he sleeps a lot. She also mentions that she misses me. The letters send me into spasms of despair. The hole of my family's absence is almost too much to bear. As is the extreme gap between what I know, what I love, and where I am.

In one of her letters, my mother recounts seeing me.

She is walking through the market when, suddenly, there I am. She calls out my name and runs after me, but the young woman who turns around isn't me. Just someone else. A young woman who looks just like me.

I picture my mother. Her dark hair, her small frame, her kind, grey eyes. She is carrying a bag of vegetables and some fruit. She has bought the cheeses I like. I picture her face as she thinks she sees me. Her arm outstretched, her wide smile, her mouth calling my name.

29

I return to Paris eight months later. A rough and long punishment, but not without its merits. According to my father, I have become less of a wild horse. Less angry. More reasonable. And my excellent grades are proof that he is right. As for the raw, snow-filled loneliness I experienced those first few months, well it can only have made me stronger. *The hardest victory is over self*, he says, quoting Aristotle. I do not tell him what I have realised. That despite a couple of friendships I eventually managed to forge, out of necessity rather than desire, I jeopardised every chance of making things better for myself. If victory there was, it was a lame one. I convinced myself I was misunderstood. It hadn't occurred to me that, despite my seventeen years on the planet, I barely understood myself.

❀   ❀   ❀

My Parisian friends are waiting for me at the Café La Palette, our regular haunt in St Germain-des-Prés. Hélène, Nadine, Sophie. As I push the door open I immediately sense that the atmosphere is different. The three of them are seated at a round table. Their hair has grown out and they wear little makeup, unlike me. My hair is frizzy, I overdo it on the makeup—a Vermont leftover. There is a thick smell of smoke in the air. My friends are puffing on Rothman cigarettes. They are laughing in unison when I arrive, and I feel self-conscious. They greet me warmly, though not effusively: I've been gone a long time.

I squeeze into a seat beside them. I order coffee and light one of Sophie's cigarettes. But I haven't had one in months, and it makes my head spin.

As the conversation progresses, I feel a palpable gap between us.

I have missed out on a whole sequence of events, especially the last year of high school: they have passed their baccalaureate; I have an American diploma instead and have been accepted by a New England college—this sets us apart. I also speak another language, which they do not. I try to pretend that nothing is different. That my brief exodus was insignificant. That I am exactly the same as when I left. But in fact I am not, and neither are they. Our adolescent selves stand at the threshold of adulthood, our future features slowly emerging from their chrysalises. We have all changed. New love affairs, breakups, parties—life changes too. Nadine's parents have divorced. It is all very recent. We talk about it briefly. It was an affair, she says, without going into specifics. It feels like a fresh wound. As if a dog had bitten her. But she'll be fine, she adds, her quivering voice betraying the power of that bite. Time to change the subject. She wants to know about boarding school—they all do. Whether the boys were cute, the girls friendly, the teachers good. I find myself extolling the institution's virtues, the landscape, the teachers, the dreaded field trips. And as I describe my American routine it occurs to me, with some surprise, that I view the experience with a hint of nostalgia rather than rancour. And this is the stance I decide to adopt. I had a great time. It was a total success. I loved it, I declare. I made nice friends. I lost my virginity to a politician's son—Bradley, a rich guy from Virginia whose father worked for the Reagan administration. Bradley dressed in Ralph Lauren and was obsessed with tennis. Really cute but so uptight. And not much fun. It did not last long. I do not tell them that I chose Bradley because he was Alexander's opposite. I thought it would help me forget him. In fact, the experience reinforced my craving. My conviction that I might never meet Alexander's equal. Or will I?

The girls are laughing about Bradley and want to know more. And as I tentatively string the pearls of our friendship back together, I understand that I cannot disclose the truth. It would somewhat tarnish the image they have of me, as an independent young woman who left her family behind in search of something different. That the words 'left her family behind' are inaccurate, and that I was in fact booted out by my father, seems to have been forgotten. What matters is that, in their eyes, I have emerged a winner. A warrior. I lived on the other side of the ocean, far away from home. I made do with the situation. I am fluent in two languages. I dress stylishly, "like a rock star". I'm going to study at an American university and I look happy. Really? Really.

And what about Alexander? Nadine, who knows everything about me, asks. Do you still think of him?

All three of them are now staring at me and it takes me a while to answer.

Not really. Only sometimes, I finally say.

We order sandwiches and more coffee. Nadine is no longer interested in Guatemala but London, where she says she would like to live. She has fallen in love with an English guitarist called John, whom she met on the ferry. Her mother is appalled. She thinks John is a drug addict because he has long hair. In fact, he's related to some Lord. But her parents don't care about Lords because they're communists. But they do care about their daughter's welfare, even if they don't love each other anymore, Nadine adds wryly. Sophie announces that she too would like to go to London. Maybe go to art school there, and perhaps or perhaps not become an artist. Then she shrugs her shoulders. Or maybe I'll stay in Paris and go to art school here. Hélène, who has always been the grandest of the four of us, nods affirmatively. I wouldn't go anywhere else, she says. Why would I? And the food in England is disgusting.

Hélène would like to study economics but has no other plans. There is no pressure on her to become anything apart from a wife, she once confessed, her voice tinged with a sense of guilty acceptance. Her family have an ancestral castle in South-West France. Their preoccupations have to do with inheritance and status. I met Hélène's mother once, a tall and elegant woman. She tried hard to suppress any hint of condescension as she took me in, and quietly ruled me out. Her daughter has never ruled me out. But, unlike Nadine and Sophie, I have not once been in-vited to spend a weekend at the 'chateau'. I've often wondered what her mother says behind my back—the Jewish girl with curly hair and intellectual parents. I know from Hélène that, according to her mother, the notion of hobnobbing with artists or intellectuals is considered a bit risqué.

I like the idea of my parents being risqué. I have never thought of them that way. Am I risqué too?

I light another cigarette, and this time my head no longer spins.

Risqué me.

30

At college I study comparative literature. A friend gives me a book of Pablo Neruda's poems. Once I begin, I cannot stop. I fall in love with him and his words.

> But I love your feet
> only because they walked
> upon the earth and upon
> the wind and upon the waters,
> until they found me.

Who will find me? Will it be Alexander?

31

I am sitting in an Upper West Side deli, eating a chicken salad sandwich on the corner of Broadway and 83rd. My uncle, my mother's elder brother, is sitting opposite me, and we're discussing my future. I care about you, my uncle says. About how your life will turn out.

He is eating an egg sandwich and there is a dollop of mayonnaise on the corner of his upper lip, but I feel shy pointing it out.

I do not know how my life will turn out. I am eighteen years old, with fiery dreams and pale confidence. I am seeking something I cannot define, something that involves knowledge. It is connected to experience, but also sensations. The dollop of mayonnaise on the corner of my uncle's lip, and my inability to point it out, is one of them. Being a freshman in college. Becoming American. When will I return to Paris? Where do I belong? How my future will pan out is an increasing concern. I still feel my parents' presence, wired inside me like some sort of implant. It keeps me from moving forward. I call them too often. They are loving. I hate their love. I want to be free. To please myself, not them. Yet I am the one who calls them. Who seeks my father's approval, still. He judges me often, just like he does my mother. I wonder whether most men are like him. If so, I will have to fight them. Prove to them that I am different. I do not want to be judged, but understood. I want my voice to be heard.

I have something to say. But every time I try to artic-
ulate my thoughts, I am overcome by a constricting
feeling, as if I were wearing a tight corset. I need
breathing space. Expansion. An invisible seamstress
is taking care of the problem. We're nearly there, she
keeps telling me. We just need to adjust the centre
seams. Make this a perfect fit.

I try to explain this to my uncle. Not about the
centre seams or the perfect fit, but my need to find
breathing space and break free from my parents. He
does not seem to understand. He is a gentle man. I
don't like the word hate, he says. And one cannot
hate love.

But I need to break away from them, I insist.

Why? He asks. Why would you want to do that?
They're your parents. They love you. What's wrong
with love?

Nothing. Nothing is wrong with love.

My inner angst is not something my uncle can relate
to. He never had a problem with his parents. He did
not flee from the constraints of his religion, or move
to another country, like my mother did. He is happy
with life as it is.

He asks for the bill, and we walk out onto the busy
street. For a long time afterwards, I think of that day.
Of his caring about how my life might turn out. I
wonder whether I will know when the turning begins.
I suspect it will coincide with that perfect fit. The fit
of me. It could take years, but it will happen. And love
has to do with it. The shaping of love. Once life and
love have shaped me, I will no longer feel stifled, but
able to take the world by storm.

32

I have gathered my author friends around my fic-
titious dining table. I serve them cold soup and a
Niçoise salad. I admire each one of them for different

reasons. I have invited Anton Chekhov, Marguerite Duras, Louis Aragon, Elsa Morante, James Salter, James Baldwin, Françoise Sagan, Virginia Woolf, and Philip Roth. It is a crowded table.

Françoise and Marguerite smoke in a corner and don't eat. They've known each other for a while and have had their differences. But they also share many similarities. Françoise is reliant on drugs, Marguerite on alcohol. The former has a more timorous personality than the latter. Marguerite is an utter narcissist, and for this reason Elsa Morante shuns her, as does Louis Aragon, who much prefers talking to Chekhov. Aragon speaks Russian well, having been a committed communist for so many years—a leaning that Chekhov, who has veered more towards socialism, does not share. They both studied medicine, although Aragon abandoned it after WWI. I tell Elsa that I think the reason why Chekhov writes so humanly is that he has been able to transpose his medical understanding of the pulse into prose. She agrees, and we discuss him further. I hope he doesn't hear us. In fact, I am secretly in love with Anton, and have been for years. I intercept James Baldwin casting a fleeting glance in his direction too. He has a wonderful voice and smokes between mouthfuls. He also has a space between his front teeth, which I find attractive. He and Philip Roth are the most humorous, while James Salter is as reserved as Virginia. She gazes ruminatively into the distance rather than at the crowd. How old is she? I wonder. The subject of drinks comes up, and James Salter says he mixes a good martini. Then James Baldwin mentions something which Virginia deems funny, and she bursts into unexpectedly contagious laughter, like a child. Soon all the English-speaking writers are laughing with Virginia, while the French ones wonder what all the fuss is about. Eventually she starts telling a story which loops into another story—and yet another. I have never heard anything like it. I am entranced by her, but need to pay attention to my other guests, especially Anton. But he is busy speaking to James Salter. I cannot hear what they are saying. Their voices are drowned by Elsa Morante, who speaks loudly. She insists on being called a *scrittore* rather than a *scrittrice* in Italy, which I admire. If I ever become a writer I would like to be called a *scrittore* too. Marguerite says she likes the idea while Philip finds it ridiculous. After dinner, drinks are served. Many cigarettes are lit, a cheroot in Virginia's case. The room fills up with smoke.

Someone open the damn window! Phillip shouts.

Then Joan Armatrading bursts through the door and belts out "Love and Affection" and everyone stops and stares. Everyone, that is, apart from Anton, who whispers in my ear that he does not like this sort of music. He much prefers Tchaikovsky or Rachmaninoff. He met Rachmaninoff in Yalta, in 1900. He thought he had a remarkable face and was destined to become a great man.

33

My boyfriend in college is called Adam. He comes from the rust belt of Ohio and has never left America. He would like to become a photographer and shows me his work: empty landscapes, car junkyards, night lights in destitute towns. I find them strong, albeit depressing.

Adam is handsome, soft spoken, and in love with me. It is unreciprocated, but I don't let him know. I need him, and love, in my life. If it cannot be Alexander, then Adam will do. Plus, I find his working-class background fascinating. My father, who visits me at college, is less impressed and treats Adam patronisingly. We argue and I reprimand him. Adam is stable. Reassuring. My father would never understand. Reassurance is not a concept he's familiar with.

For my junior year abroad, Adam follows me to Paris where I find an apartment in the Bastille. Through some contacts I land him a job working in a photographer's studio. The photographer encourages him to go out and capture the city. Soon enough, Adam's desolate landscapes are swapped for Parisian street scenes: furtive lovers, café tables, portraits of me and some of my friends. Although good, there is a certain flatness about them. When I try to explain, as gently as I can, that he should delve deeper, Adam gets very upset. Who do you think you are? Delve deeper into what, exactly? Your snootiness?

His childish reaction upsets me. It is the first of many such episodes. Increasingly I go out without him. By day I study at the Sorbonne, by night I go to parties, where I reconnect with my old friends. Adam says it suits him fine. He doesn't like parties anyway. But, in fact, there is a language barrier. A cultural and social one too. I realise that I might be mistreating him. I take his love for granted. I want him to challenge me, but he doesn't.

34

I am celebrating my twenty-first birthday with friends in an Italian restaurant. The waiters are Portuguese. Andy Warhol has just died. Freddie Mercury has admitted he has AIDS, and Serge Gainsbourg has released a new song, "Gloomy Sunday". I wear a short black dress and vermilion lipstick. Adam says he doesn't like it when I wear lipstick. I don't care what you think, I retort. He is hurt and leaves in a huff. I pretend not to notice. After dinner I will dance the night away at the Bains Douches. Perhaps Mick Jagger will be there. He was spotted last time, as was Yves Saint Laurent. I wish I could afford his clothes. Instead I shop in flea markets, drink strong coffee, and eat croque monsieur for lunch—crunch the man.

35

I attend the lecture of the great Professor R. at the Sorbonne. Held in one of the oldest conference rooms, it is a coveted affair, attended by eager hordes of participants. His passion is as infectious as his knowledge. I am especially drawn to the post-war *nouveaux romans*, to those writers who broke away from tradition: I like it when rules are broken. The words flow free and fresh. Unstoppable. I can hear the sentences breathe. Pant. I would like to observe rather than interpret, just like them. Observe with the precision of a microscope. Can I do it? The great professor has triggered something in me. He doesn't know who I am. He will never know the impact his words have on me or how, one day, coming out of one of his classes, it will suddenly hit me: this is my calling. I see life from different angles. I would like to write about that.

The angles.

I get a job translating articles for a museum in Paris. I often come across André Karlick's name. Every time I do my heart burns for Alexander.

What does he look like? Where is he?

36

It is a bit of a surprise, the realisation that I am stuck in the same creative, monomaniacal mire that I fought so hard to extricate myself from: the universe of words. Then again, I will be doing things differently. I refute the purist values that were drummed into me. I am not a purist. I am not like my parents. I do not seal myself into the comfort of what I know. But that doesn't detract from the fact that there is something inherently solipsistic about sitting at a desk and listening to one's voice creating its own world. And in fact, when I try to express myself, nothing comes out. Only wisps of evanescent thought. An invisible barrier stands between me and the flow of my pen. I do not know how long the evanescence will last. When the barrier will fall.

37

New York, 1992

I have finished college. I work in a bookshop in the West Village with Paola, an Italian biologist. She comes from a conservative Milanese family. Like me, she has found her freedom in New York. Our favourite hunting grounds are Cafe La Fortuna, on the Upper West Side, and Caffé Dante on Macdougal Street. In the evenings we go out dancing, sometimes until the early hours. Paola never seems tired. I have a lot of *enerrgy*, she boasts, with her trademark Italian accent. She is spirited, bright, and fiercely ambitious. She also harbours dreams of getting married and having children, which sets her apart—no one I know at the time speaks of such things. Yet she does. It's what I want, she says. To meet the man of my dreams, get married, and have children.

Adam is not a fan of Paola's. He finds her too loud. Doesn't like the fact that we spend so much time together. But he still loves me. I didn't think the relationship would last this long, but it has. There is something about him that makes me reluctant to leave him. Is it guilt, or something else? I cannot tell, but I know that the answer will eventually come to me.

38

I am at graduate school, studying English literature.
I am writing my thesis on Paul Éluard, the French poet. I am also writing about a young woman who has stepped into my thoughts. I call her Marie. I have broken through the barrier between my voice and the flow of my pen. The words whirl like wind inside my head and become a story. Then another. I have bridged the gap between page and person. I light a cigarette, the first of many. Now a cacophony of voices joins Marie. I write frantically. The curled corners of my pages are dark with coffee stains and

cigarette ash. It is a matter of filtering through the cacophony. I light another cigarette in order to focus on my quest. Adam hates the smell. We argue until he gives way.

You can smoke in the kitchen with the window open. But it really stinks. And I don't think cigarettes will help you find your voice, he adds, sounding snide.

What do you know? I ask him. What do you know about voice?

Plenty more than you think, he snaps back.

39

Adam and I live in a pre-war building on Barrow Street, between a hardware shop and an Italian café that always looks empty.

I am increasingly disillusioned with him. I am not in love with him, never have been, although I would have liked to be. We argue a lot. I don't even bother asking him to join me in the evening anymore. I have a new set of friends, and he doesn't fit in. Nor does he seem to want to. He can feel my growing impatience with him, I can tell.

But he still chooses to say nothing.

40

I go to parties in Soho lofts and walk-up buildings in the East Village. Once Adam accompanies me. He hovers in the background and drinks beer. I like to watch, not belong, he tells me. I have you and that's plenty. That's why I don't need to go anywhere.

At one of those parties I kiss another man. He asks me back to his place, but my conscience gnaws at me.

I think of Adam, waiting for me. The man who does not like to belong.

I cannot do it.

There is a corner shop near us which is tended by an Afghan man called Kabir. He has dark skin and green eyes, and there is something majestic about him. He sells everything from dry foods to dairy products, as well as fruit and vegetables and, most days of the week, fresh flowers. There is often Afghan music playing on a small radio. Sometimes I hear him humming along with it. Once I caught him with his eyes closed. A woman's voice was singing a mournful melody. Kabir was tilting his head slowly, from side to side. Then, just as I was about to greet him, I saw tears roll down his cheeks. They were still closed as I quietly left.

42

In the back of Kabir's shop there is Aleppo pepper, cardamom, and turmeric. Pistachios, almonds, liquorice, dates, and sundried apricots. There are also cigarettes, bottles of liquor, barley and rice, mint and coriander. Some of these things remind him of home, he tells me. Kabir comes from the Farah Province, in the southwestern part of Afghanistan. He came to the US in 1979, after the Soviet invasion. His children were small, his wife was pregnant. He sometimes dons an embroidered woollen cap that was given to him by his father, a Pashtun tribesman. Kabir dreams of returning to his country but isn't sure when he will.

My feet are in Flushing, but my heart is in Farah, he says. In my country we say that even on a mountain there is still a road. I can see that mountain, but not always the road, he laughs.

His children, who are more American than he will ever be, have only visited their parents' homeland once. They don't like speaking Farsi in public. They don't care whether Afghanistan is a beautiful country. All that matters to them is to belong. Because

America is so bewitching, it can dissolve a whole slice of history in one generation, Kabir says. And my children have been bewitched.

I do not tell him that the bewitchment he's referring to is freedom. In that sense I've been bewitched too. My circumstances may be very different—I do not come from a war-torn country, nor do I sell fruit and vegetables in a corner shop—but a sense of displacement unites us. I have swapped one country for another. I too wonder about that mountain road. About the language of exile. About preserving my history. I would like to tell Kabir that the only way forward is to live life outside what one knows—until the outside eases into the inside.

43

Adam rarely shops at Kabir's. When he does—for a pint of milk, bread, or coffee—he does not engage in conversation with the man behind the counter. To him, Kabir is just a polite and pleasant shopkeeper who is doing his job, as thousands of others like him do. Adam is not interested in his flight from the Farah province to the corner of West 4th Street. In the way Kabir has attempted to adapt his old life to his current surroundings. The concept of coming from somewhere else is not one that preoccupies Adam. It's about the now, he often tells me. Making the best of the now—and making it better. That's why he's a photographer. Because he likes to freeze-frame the moment. What happened before is immaterial.

To me, what happened before is everything.

44

My mother grew up in Odessa, Ukraine. She has distant memories of a house on a tree-lined street. A red dress she wore on special occasions. The smell of blooming acacias in the springtime.

Her aunt and uncle lived three houses down with their five children. Every morning she walked to school with her brothers and cousins. A long line of us, like working ants, is how she described it.

In June 1941 German and Romanian troops invaded Odessa. My mother was nine years old at the time. The city was bombed, and the air was filled with smoke and soot. A beautiful summer's day which turned to soot. She has never forgotten how the sky lost its colour. How her father announced that the family had to leave. We can no longer stay here, he said. Her father had always been a wise man. Whatever he said carried weight. But her uncle refused to listen. My grandfather pleaded with him, but his brother was stubborn. This is my life, he said. I will not let anyone interrupt it. I am not leaving.

My grandmother reassured the children that all was going to be well. It was only a temporary departure. That they would return home. They would be reunited with their possessions, their friends.

Of course they would return home.

They left in the middle of the night. A tall man her grandfather knew knocked on their door. They were told to follow him. My mother remembers the darkness. Following the tall man she had never met before. They walked carrying their belongings in silence. She can still remember that silence. The terror of breaking it. The terror of the unknown. I picture my mother's cold bed after she was ordered to leave.

What happened after their departure? How long did those beds remain empty? Did other people move in, or was the house destroyed?

It happened very quickly. A matter of minutes, my mother said. We had a home and then we didn't. Everything we knew disappeared. Just like that, she said, snapping her fingers.

Just like that.

A few months later, her aunt, uncle, and their five children were all deported to a concentration camp. None of them came back alive.

I think of empty beds all over the world and the rubble of war. War beds. Forced displacement and cold sheets. How long it takes for normality to descend into hell.

A few minutes, at most. Men, women, and children being wrenched away while a house is left behind, alive with ghostly whispers.

The fragile veneer of civilisation.

45

On the Lower East Side there were no special occasions or blooming acacias. My grandparents clung to the two things that mattered most: religion and language. This enabled them to conduct their lives as they had always done: as if time had stood still. And in fact, their neighbourhood was filled with families like them, all living as if time had stood still. As if modernity hadn't reached their windowpanes. But my mother was different. A new voice was infiltrating her, like a ventriloquist. She liked the sound of that voice. Its flavour. Its temperature. That small girl with the red dress was left behind. A woman from somewhere else took her place. The transition was initially unsteady, until it became part of her identity.

My mother said later that this is what led her to become a translator. Recreating the original. Transferring one vision into a different language. Like navigating between two continents on one ship.

46

Displacement: "the act of moving someone or something from one position to another or the measurement of the volume replaced by something else". In French, displacement is translated as *déracinement*—to be wrenched away from one's roots or the familiar—or *dépaysement*, which is the rendering I prefer.

Decountried. Disorientated. Lost. A long journey of forcefully separated pieces. Of memory split asunder. We are made of chiaroscuro: pools of light and fleeting shadows.

47

I run towards the subway. Despite the dark, the West Village is ablaze with cherry blossoms. I am late for a party. A plume of steam rises up from a manhole cover. On 14th Street, a Chinese dry cleaner is arguing with a customer outside his shop. I am dressed in black—I always am: black cowboy boots, black jeans, a striped black and white T-shirt, and a black leather jacket.

The party is in a Soho loft, between Prince Street and Broadway.

I meet up with Claudia. She is speaking to a poet with long hair who is smoking a joint. Other friends of ours show up, eager to move on to the next party. This one is a bit boring, they say. We hear the other one is better. I don't particularly want to leave, but follow them nonetheless. It takes a while to get there, as no one is entirely sure of the address.

I find it, somewhere in Alphabet City. The building looks derelict, covered in graffiti. A young man with black, matted hair is slumped against the door of an adjacent building, but everyone ignores him.

Do you think he's all right? Claudia asks me.

I don't know.

I look at him quickly. His arm covers his face. His trousers look wet. Something about him makes me shiver. Come, says Claudia. There's nothing we can do about him.

I follow her up a few flights of stairs. The man throwing the party is a student from Parsons School of Design. His arm is covered in tattoos. The party is in full swing. Claudia mentions the young man lying downstairs. He's a junkie, the student says. He lives in the squat next door. He's some rich kid, off his head most of the time.

I don't ask further questions.

I drink and smoke and talk to writers, painters, and budding film directors.

I forget about where I am, how I got there, about Adam waiting for me at home. My future stretches out in front of me, filled with endless possibilities. I inhale them, swim in their scent, sweet like honeysuckle. I am free, young, attractive. I love New York and its energy. I could do anything and no one would care. I drink more beer, the music is turned up, and we all begin to dance to a Talking Heads song. *Qu'est-ce que c'est | Fa-fa-fa-fa-fa-fa-fa-fa-fa-far better.* I kiss another man, Noah. *Run run run run run run away.*

He asks me to join him and his friends at Danceteria. Yes, I will join them. I leave the loft and see that the junkie is gone, but a piece of his clothing remains.

Poor guy, I remark. I hope he's OK.

He's not OK, one of Noah's friends tells me. He's pretty fucked up. I kinda knew him a few years ago. We went to NYU together. He's the son of that gallery owner, the rich guy whose wife jumped out of a window.

Holy fuck, Claudia says.

I stop in my tracks and ask him to repeat the information, just to be sure.

What? Do you mean Alexander Karlick?

Yeah, that's him. I knew him as Alex. He's really smart. Then he got into heroin.

I begin to tremble from head to toe. I run back and pick up the piece of clothing he left behind. It is a soaked and soiled T-shirt. I hold it between my fingers, longer than I should, then drop it back where I found it. This is what Alexander has become, then. Soiled, soaked in grief, abandoned. This is how he has chosen to numb the pain of his mother's death. His beautiful mother. No one standing there beside me knows the arc of Alexander's story—but I do. I know what he was like as a young boy, seven years back. I know where he lived and what the view outside his bedroom window looked like. I know how brilliant and passionate he was. I know that he could have taken the world by storm. And I know the woman who interrupted his flight. Lorna Karlick, born in Auschwitz, 1945. I think of my father's words: she couldn't live with her history.

And now it is happening to her son. He cannot live with his either. All he can do is hush her memory in a haze of heroin.

I'm about to cry. I'm in a state of utter disarray. Everyone can see it.

Do you know him? someone asks.

Yes. I did. I do. In my mind, I've always known Alexander. And now I need to find him. I'm about to rush back towards the building but am held back.

You really don't want to be going in there, man, Noah declares. It's pretty heavy shit. Especially now, at this hour.

I don't care. And he's no rich kid gone bad. He's the most amazing guy I ever met.

I'm sure he is, says Noah, but I can't let you go into that squat alone. If you do, you might never come out.

At Danceteria I get very drunk. I don't remember getting home. I think Noah put me in a cab. That's what Adam told me later. That a cab driver delivered me to the front door. Someone must have stuck you in there, he says.

I throw up. I spend the rest of the morning throwing up. Seldom have I felt so ill.

I must find Alexander. I must save him.

Tell me how you kiss.

48

It takes a few days before I am able to return to the squat. I have some exams to hand in, an essay to write.

As soon as it's completed, I jump on a subway with Adam. I've brought him along, but he's not happy. I don't like it around here, he says. It's dangerous. We could get mugged. What the fuck are we doing here?

We are standing on the corner of Avenue C and 10th Street. Adam is right: it looks like an ominous no-man's land, even more so in daylight. A menacing-looking man stares at the two of us as we walk quickly past him. Hey yo' dissin' me man? he asks, before breaking into smoke-filled laughter.

Adam grabs my hand, and we accelerate our pace. You're going to get us fucking killed here, he mutters.

It's going to be OK, I reply, trying to sound reassuring. In fact I feel as terrified as he does. But I must not show it, no matter what. If I do, he'll drag me home before I can find Alexander. And I must find him.

Or must I?

As I approach the derelict building, I start to waver. Is it really my place to go and search for a man with whom I've only spent a couple of hours of my life? Perhaps it isn't, I reason. I cannot be responsible for the choices Alexander has made. Perhaps it isn't for me to save him.

A young woman walks past us. She wears a long flowing skirt and Birkenstock sandals. She is carrying a dirty supermarket bag. Her eyes look glazed. She walks towards the squat. She knows Alexander. I can feel it in my bones. Maybe they even slept together. I stop her and she looks worried. Hey get off me! I might have touched her arm; she didn't like that.

Sorry, I say quickly. I'm looking for Alex Karlick. Do you know him? I need to speak to him.

I don't like calling him Alex. To me he'll always be Alexander. But for her sake, I must.

The woman looks at me and hesitates. Yeah. He moved out yesterday. His father came to get him. He had a big fucking car.

His father...

Yeah, she repeats. A big fucking car. Like what the fuck?

She sounds as if her mouth were full.

I hope he's going to be OK now, I whisper.

I could have been speaking to him.

The young woman has gone. I remain standing on the pavement with Adam.

What's going on? he asks me, sounding upset. What's this Alex shit about anyway? The loser who lives in a squat, right?

Lived in a squat. No longer. And he was never a loser.

OK well who is he? Do you love the guy or what?

I don't know, I answer quietly. I honestly don't know.

After we return home that evening, Adam announces that he is moving out.

I've had it with you. I don't want anything more to do with you. You're not a nice person. I'm sorry it took me so long to see it.

49

I feel guilty. I saw him cry when he was packing. I went to hug him, but he pushed me away. What he said about me not being a nice person isn't true: I am. It was his indolence that made me meaner. After he left, I felt a small void, but it quickly dissipated. Adam was a good man, just not the right one for me. But perhaps I needed him more than I realised. Perhaps I liked it that someone was there, waiting for me every time I returned home from my dancing nights. And perhaps he needed my presence too, even if I could not love him as he wanted me to.

50

I throw parties in my apartment, where I serve cheap wine and Italian cheese from nearby Balducci's. I buy the liquor at Kabir's, and he gives me a large box of dried fruit and nuts as a gift. I ask him if he'd like to come to one of my parties. With your wife, of course, I add. He smiles and says he's very sorry, but it won't be possible. But he's most touched I asked him, he says. Most touched.

When I see him again his attitude towards me is different. Slightly colder. I understand that inviting Kabir to my party was a mistake. Perhaps he saw something patronising in my wishing to include the green-eyed vegetable man in my life. Kabir does not wish to be part of my life. A tacit demarcation line existed between us all along, one he wanted to maintain. By treating him as a friend I broke that line. Eventually the awkwardness became such that I stopped shopping there altogether.

51

I cook dinner for a few friends from graduate school. David is a writer in one of my classes. He is talented, intelligent, Jewish. I haven't had many Jewish boyfriends. Alexander was Jewish but he was never my boyfriend. And I must not be thinking about Alexander anymore. He is an addict. Even if his father has saved him, he is still an addict. Addiction frightens me. I would not know how to cope with it or its aftermath. I hold on to the image I have of the adolescent Alexander Karlick instead. The one that made my heart break into shards of longing and love. Not the man I found lying on a Manhattan pavement, somewhere between dusk and dawn.

I still have a notebook from that time. I found a page on which these words were scribbled:

The St Mark's bookshop, in the East village.
The coffee stain on p.87 of 'Tender is the night'.
Twenty-three years old. Smoking a cigarette and not
    liking wine.
Men.

Different beds. Broken hearts.

Bonnard and Matisse.

Dancing to Talking Heads.

Vermilion apples in the market.

The way the world feels at twenty-three years old.

Guerlain perfume.

Alexander's eyes. Will they ever lock into mine again?

The smell of streets. A pair of black velvet ankle boots.

The way my mother applies lipstick. Her lips rounded into a *shh*. The way my father crinkles his nose when he reads.

Finding the right balance between the life I know and the life I want.

52

I read an interview with Natalia Ginzburg, published just before her death in 1991. *I write about families because that is where everything starts, where the germs grow.*

I meet my husband at a party. I believe in synchronicity, he tells me. In alchemy. You've alchemised me.

I find myself besotted with him. He is handsome, intelligent, different from the other men I've met until then. There is something exotic about him, like a Siamese cat.

I love your eyes. I love your voice. I love everything about you, he says.

53

I introduce him to my parents. They immediately comment on the intelligence, his good looks, the fact that he is English. My father is thrilled. He has always had a penchant for Englishmen.

I marry the Englishman and move to London. He explains that New York was never going to be long term. Nor had it been an entirely positive experience for him. But he met me there, and that means everything. He has a new job lined up in Canary

Wharf, the job of his dreams. I do not know Canary Wharf or any of the neighbourhoods he refers to, and although I am pleased for him, the move makes me nervous: unlike my new husband's, my stay in New York has been a positive one, and I hardly know London. What if I don't like it? I think of my mother's words. You must make the best of it, darling. You'll have such a wonderful time there. Even if it's a bit hard in the beginning, I'm sure you'll grow to love it. And your husband is at your side. All he will want is for his wife to be happy.

❀   ❀   ❀

I spend a lot of time walking around London with a map, like a tourist. When I'm not walking, I ride buses. I sit by the window and watch neighbourhoods appear and disappear. The spire of St Martin-in-the-Fields. The elegant houses of Holland Park. A man selling scarves on the corner of Theobalds Road. Two small Indian girls holding hands in Piccadilly. The green of their mother's sari and the way it flutters in the wind as they cross the street. The cherry blossoms in Tavistock Square. The way the petals float to the ground like confetti. A homeless man lying in front of a church door in Mayfair. The black soles of his bare feet. A well-dressed couple walking quickly. Schoolchildren in striped uniforms crossing Regent's Park Road. I've never seen children wearing uniforms before. I find that it makes it harder to distinguish their ages. Or perhaps that is because I don't know much about children. I haven't given them much thought. But my husband has. He says he would like one soon. One only, no more. A boy, maybe. A boy would be nice. But I'm not ready yet. I would like to spend more time alone with him. We married quickly. There is still a lot we don't know about each other.

The city grows on me, especially North London. But my husband likes the West better. I know no one

in North London, he says. It's where all the elite lefties live. And I don't like elite lefties.

At a bus stop one day I meet Julia, a sociologist, who
ends up becoming a friend. Through her I meet other
academics, and eventually my group widens. I also
spend time at the French Institute, as an acquaint-
ance from Paris works there. A social life helps to ease
my transition into London. My husband is different.
There is no transition required. His social life re-
volves around two friends from university, whom he
sees occasionally. He says that he only does so because
they insist. I have you and that's plenty, he tells me. I
don't really need to spend time with anyone else.

We live in a purpose-built block of flats near the
Edgware Road. There is one bedroom and a small
living room, both of which are fitted with ugly grey
carpets. As it faces north there is little light. At first
I don't mind because I am happy. Besides, I have
never given much thought to where I live. I am used
to small rental apartments. My parents have never
owned their own place, nor is it something they have
ever contemplated.

I fall pregnant and give birth to Katia. Not a boy. But
my husband is happy. Caring. Then after a few weeks
he goes back to work. A new contract, something to
do with China. I find myself alone. Childbirth and
its after-effects incapacitate me. I begin to resent
that grey carpet, the lack of light. But I cannot afford
to move elsewhere. Not yet. Soon, my husband promises. But soon is slow to come and hostility begins to
gather pace. It knocks into me, making me stumble.
But I will do nothing about it. Even if I wanted to, I
wouldn't know where to start. I believe the saying
that love conquers all.

54

I find that he is hard to please, quick to anger. The

job in Canary Wharf only lasts four months before he is fired. Unfairly, he argues. Something to do with that Chinese contract. He is offered a position elsewhere. He admits that, until he met me, the notion of steadiness had always been anathema to him. I've moved around a lot, he says. Playing cards is the one distraction which he has stuck to over the years. Where I go, my cards follow, he jokes.

Now he works for a Germany-based games company with a UK subsidiary. He has become the head of the UK branch, and although the salary is low, his enthusiasm for the gaming industry is high. Mine is not. But that is probably because his is a world I do not understand, nor do I particularly wish to. In turn he has no interest in books, although he proclaims himself a history buff. It's all about life, not books, he says. And history is life. Novels are only its reflection.

Our marriage is therefore about finding an overlap, like in a Venn diagram. One that we can both inhabit comfortably without feeling that something is missing.

❉   ❉   ❉

His childhood was a parched one. The opposite of mine. Everything about my husband's background is the opposite of mine. What I misconstrued as exoticism is in fact an act, born out of necessity. The desire to escape from the aridity of his past.

I had to flee, he says. Away from the darkness at home. Make my own life. I'm still making it.

I do not know the full arc of his story. All I know is that his father was a cold man and his mother a victim of that coldness. Where does this place my husband? I met him in the middle of things, after the arc's trajectory had already been determined. Both his trajectory and mine. After it was too late to stop it.

Where the germs grow.

He has tense relations with his parents, whom he rarely sees. He confesses that the notion of spending time with them fills him with dread rather than pleasure. They still live where he grew up, in a 1950s house in Surrey. I visited twice, and on both occasions his mother wore a fixed smile on her face and stared at me blankly, as if she had barely noticed me. Her conversation was limited to banalities: the weather, the dog, and how travelling to London had become frightful. So many foreigners, she said. Too many foreigners. She asked me no questions, sought no answers as to what had drawn a young Parisian woman to her son in the first place. I would have felt insulted if it wasn't for the fact that something about her felt amiss. As if she were unhinged. When I queried my husband, he admitted that there were issues. Something wasn't right with his mother. Hadn't been for a long while. This is where the dread came from. His father knew it too. That her behaviour was abnormal. The staring into the void. The refusal to communicate. But this was not a normal family. They did not believe in confrontation or in addressing uncomfortable issues, especially not if they had to do with mental health.

The light has gone out of my mother, my husband said. And there is nothing we can do to switch it on again.

There were attempts to take her to a psychiatrist. But his mother wouldn't hear of it. Shouted that there was nothing wrong with her. Threatened to leave the house forever if they insisted. The only time she seemed normal again.

My husband blames his father, a weak man. Too weak to take this on. He would rather remain weak than challenge his wife. Seek help for her. But that is probably because he does not really care. He never really loved her. There was another woman.

This made his wife suffer. For years she had to put up with the affair. Another child, possibly. Now she's forgotten it ever happened.

At our wedding his parents sat together, barely engaging with anyone. His mother drank too many glasses of wine while his father pretended not to notice. He had white hair and long fingers, like snakes.
My husband has inherited his fingers.

56

I have been married five years. My mother-in law has died and, with his modest inheritance, my husband has bought a two-bedroom, first-floor flat in Hammersmith, facing our neighbour's garden. Although it isn't a large space, it is lighter and more comfortable than our previous one. And I enjoy the garden view. How certain flowers bloom at certain times. My husband knows about flowers, and soon I begin to recognise them. Phlox. Irises. Foxgloves. Delphiniums. Names which were never part of my vocabulary before. His mother liked to garden, one of the only fond memories he has of her. He remembers helping her as an adolescent. Weeding and planting seeds. Mowing the lawn. The smell of freshly cut grass. The feel of earth between his fingers. That was before I began to hate my parents, he tells me. Before they turned into horrible people.

I don't know what to say to that. I often don't. I wish he had had a happier childhood. I wonder whether his parents really were that horrible. Increasingly, I wish I had known more about him before marrying him. My husband's words often take me by surprise. His actions too.

Soon after we moved into our new flat, with one-year-old Katia in tow, I received a sizeable advance for my new novel. I was happy. With the move, with the fact that Katia was finally sleeping through the night, and that my work was being praised. Things were looking up. But not for my husband. He no longer worked for the German company and could not seem to find another job. This made him tense. Those romantic words that had once peppered our conjugal vocabulary eventually dried up. So did intimacy. The overlap we had sought never fully materialized. The two of us ended up surviving on my teaching salary and my book advance, and he resented me for it. He did not admit it, but I could feel it. In the sharp pinch of his words. The stony glares. The card games he played alone. The cascading sound of his nocturnal shuffle. The accumulation of empty wine bottles. The incipient anger rising like magma. I was thriving when he was not. There was a flurry of excitement about my novel, while he had nothing to show for himself. This is what he said to me.

I have nothing to show for myself.

Cracks appeared in our marriage. Where once they were small and faint, I could see them clearly now. I needed to keep them from spreading.

❊   ❊   ❊

It happened on my way home. I was carrying a heavy load of groceries from a nearby shop. I had friends coming over that evening for dinner. Anything to distract my husband and maintain a modicum of normality in my life. I had bought a chicken, fruit, vegetables, and a cake from a nearby bakery.

I started to cross the road that ran parallel to our street. And that's when I saw Katia, who had just turned four, crossing that same road towards me, alone.

I shouted her name, but she didn't respond. I ran towards her and dropped the bags in the middle of the road. The chicken fell out, followed by the apples and a few loose potatoes. Milk spilling white against the dark tarmac. Smashed yogurt pots. The collapsed cake.

A car screeched to a halt in front of me and I fell.

Not because it had hit me, but out of fear. Fear made me fall. The driver came out and started shouting.

What were you thinking, lady? What were you thinking?

By then a few passers-by had gathered around me. Are you OK? they asked repeatedly. Would you like us to call an ambulance?

I shook my head. No ambulance. Just my daughter. My little girl. I saw her crossing the road alone, I said, pointing into the distance. This was why I had leapt out into the traffic. I wanted to stop her. I saw my four-year-old daughter crossing the road, I repeated, in a hoarse voice.

I could tell by the way people were looking at me that they thought something was wrong. A woman walked towards me and knelt by my side as if I were a child. Can I help? she asked. There was something syrupy about her voice, and I vaguely remember declining her offer.

Two women gathered up the food for me, putting it back in the bags. One of them had ripped. Someone helped me up. I felt breathless. My legs were trembling. I had seen something that wasn't there. That was a sign of madness. Yes, there had been a girl, but she wasn't that small, she wasn't alone—and she wasn't my daughter. Her mother was walking behind rather than beside her, I was told. Perhaps that is why I had got confused?

I don't know, I replied. I really don't know.

The driver was speaking to me, but I couldn't focus on his words. I'm fine, I said to him.

I'm fine.

He eventually left. The two women who were holding me up helped me across the street and offered to take me home. But I couldn't go home. Not yet. I didn't want my husband to see me in this state. I didn't want him to know what had happened.

I found myself asking the women if they had a cigarette. Yes, one of them did. By then I had found a bench and was sitting down. My legs had stopped trembling. I was no longer breathless. The Indian man from the nearby corner shop (who presumably had seen everything) came out onto the street to give me a new plastic bag for my groceries. Something about him reminded me of Kabir. His kindness, his grace. When I first met my husband, I went in to say goodbye, to tell him that I was leaving. It felt important to do so. But instead of Kabir I found his wife sitting behind the counter. She smiled wanly and said that he would be in the following day, and yes of course she would pass on the message.

I've often wondered if she ever did.

The woman lit my cigarette and I thanked her. Now it was my hand that was shaking. She and her friend asked if there was anything else they could do. There wasn't, I said.

I thanked them again and they left.

I sat on that bench smoking, trying to control my shaking hand. The weather had turned, and a thin, sharp rain had started to fall. There was a graze on my knee from the fall. I wasn't sure how or when I was going to make it home. I was very worried about what had happened. I could not understand it. Had I suffered a hallucination? How could I have imagined that Katia had been crossing the road? Of course she hadn't. My daughter was at home, just back from school. She was in her lilac bedroom with the slanted roof. She was probably sitting at her desk drawing something. A house most likely. Drawing a house with people inside while her mother was sitting on a bench a few streets away, smoking alone in the rain.

Eventually I managed to gather my strength and went home.

I walked through the front door and put the bags of food in the kitchen.

Katia! I shouted, and she rushed down the stairs.

I hugged her tightly against me, so tightly that she winced. You're hurting me! she cried out.

I asked her where her father was. In his study, she said, on an important phone call. He had asked not to be disturbed.

I started to chop vegetables while, inside me, rocks were falling. I could hear my husband's voice in the distance. I was worried I might cut my finger because my hand was still shaking a little and the rocks were still falling.

I smiled when my daughter described a game she had played at school that morning. I smiled when, a few minutes later, my husband walked through the door. I pretended that all was well. Pretence was a trait I had mastered at an early age. I rode its waves. I navigated its currents.

I held my breath under its surface.

57

I never told anyone what happened that day, because I feared what it might reveal about my state of mind. But, for a long time afterwards, I wondered about the significance of the incident.

I could never forget the look on those faces around me when I had pointed at my supposed daughter on the street. The way that woman had knelt beside me—not as if I were a child, I decided, but mentally unstable. This is what she was thinking: that I was in the throes of a delusion. That I had to be managed with care.

This was not the first time my mind had played tricks on me. It had happened when Katia was born, and now again. Was I indeed unstable? Or was this a psychological, rather than a neurological, phenomenon? Something about the fear I harboured for my child, but also something else: I could never forgive myself for what I had done when Katia was six weeks old—and neither could my husband. It had broken the trust between us. This is what he had told me.

And although with the years that trust was rebuilt, his words lingered, leaving behind a small, indelible stain. I often woke up at night dreaming that I had done it again. And in the background, there was always my husband, looming.

58

We went to Morocco for Easter. One of the few foreign trips we took together—my husband was not a keen traveller. I bought two large, old clay pots from an antique shop in Marrakech's Medina. The owner had a beard and glasses with smudged lenses. He offered us mint tea while he fumbled with an ancient credit card machine. He promised the pots would turn up three weeks later. My husband did not trust him. You'll never see those pots again, he declared. These people are unreliable.

His words shook me. Please don't say that when the man is standing right there. Please.

He doesn't know what unreliable means. And I know I'm right, he added, in a lower voice. I just know it.

Well, I think you're wrong. I trust this man and I know that I will see those pots again. Mark my words.

I don't mark words. You do.

The man with the glasses looked at us both. You want or you don't want?

I could see he did not like my husband, who eventually capitulated. It's your money, not mine, he said. Why should I care?

Three weeks later, on the dot, a Moroccan driver in a battered truck rang our doorbell.

He was wearing sandals, which left a trail of sand behind him. He had come via Santander, he explained. He brought the pots into the house and carefully set them down in our living room.

When I unwrapped them, I found sheets of a 1982

Arabic newspaper inside. It smelled of cloves and musk. I inhaled that scented history, trying to picture the face of the man who had last read it. It had to have been a man. He was sitting in a café, in the Medina. There was a smell of orange blossom in the air. Around him, children were playing. A call to prayer echoed from a towering minaret. The man folded the paper and set off for the mosque.

59

I have been teaching creative writing at the same university for many years.

I especially enjoy my Monday classes, which are attended by eager students. Recently one of them, Amaya, a young and attractive woman from Sri Lanka, has proven to have such unmistakable talent that I have shown her work to my agent, who has taken her on. The result has been, as he has put it, explosive. Amaya has landed herself a book deal for an eye-watering sum, one much greater than I have ever made—and probably ever will make.

I can't believe any of this is happening, she told me. I can't believe that people want to pay to read me. I really can't. The emotion is too strong.

She meant it. Her whole body was shaking. She grabbed my hand and thanked me, again and again, as she had already done several times.

I am thrilled for her. But I cannot pretend that Amaya's success hasn't affected me in some way. Suddenly this young woman I have encouraged and nurtured since I first read her has stepped into a league that far surpasses mine. It has created an imbalance, but one of which she is apparently unaware. She continues to attend my classes and participate in the workshops. Once or twice I've been tempted to discuss her style with her. What it is that makes it so much more enticing than mine, for example. When Amaya writes, flowers bloom on the page. Food sizzles. East

Sri Lankan waves rise dangerously between the lines. And she is only twenty-four years old. I am about to turn forty. I write stories which replicate my life. Motherhood, marital strife, real estate longings. I buy myself a house in France where I shelter from the marital winds. Just like when I was a teenager, I take a lover and eat dinner in small Bourguignon restaurants with white tablecloths and French folk songs playing in the background. But this lover drinks too much, and I leave France for Spain without him. I start again. I am perpetually on the run.

The story gets published in a renowned magazine. But there is something more I could be writing. It is just a matter of finding it. Stories are found, not made up.

60

Amaya's story is about luck. Talent. The possibility of stardom. *When preparation meets opportunity.* Never, when I was younger, would I have imagined that the opportunity might come from me. But it has. And the excitement is contagious. I cannot stop it from spreading. What started in the comfort of my classroom is on its way to becoming a worldwide, bestselling phenomenon. Amaya will soon leave my classroom and move to the US, where she has been offered a residency for the following year. She trembles as she imparts the news to me. Her emotions are palpable. Moving. I will never forget you, she says.

61

My husband has lost an important client. Katia is watching Paddington Bear on television and pretends not to hear him shout. I know what will happen next. The air will clog up with his fumes. I have become the recipient of his anger, the repository of his unhappiness. His skin is taut and stretched. If I were to touch it, it would feel hard, like a drum. Katia will continue to watch Paddington Bear amidst the fumes. The cycle of my husband's moods is unbreakable.

And, increasingly, I don't feel like touching him.

Useless woman, he says to me that night. That's all you are. A useless woman.

I don't know why I married you. Biggest mistake I ever made. Biggest.

62

Shortly after my first novel was published I was invited to attend a literary festival in Barcelona, where I was going to be in discussion with a celebrated writer. Accommodation and flights had been paid for by the organisers, who sent me a detailed schedule covering those four days: interviews, lunches, dinners, tours of the city. I was looking forward to it. Before I left, and because I had pressed the issue, my husband had expressed mild interest in joining me. This made me happy. Really? Do you really want to come? Then he changed his mind, and, although I wasn't surprised, it didn't stop me from being upset. He hardly ever attended my events. Of all my appearances, this one meant the most to me. I was going to be in discussion with a celebrated writer. I would have liked him to be there. To be proud of me. He seldom was these days. Perhaps this might even revivify our ailing marriage? That alchemy we once shared? He had finally found a new job. The salary was high. The stress levels had dropped. So had the abusive language. He wanted peace, he claimed. So I had ventured that being away for a few days amongst inspiring strangers might do us both good.

Not all strangers are inspiring, my husband had replied. And yes, I found a new job, and have a lot of work to do. You go and have a good time. I'll look after Katia.

I would have really liked you to come, I repeated. I thought this would be a nice thing for us to do together. Something different, for a change.

My husband looked at me. But it's not different, is it? It's all about you, not me. No change there.

I guess so, I said. I guess it's all about me. I'm sorry. Sometimes I'm even sorry I exist, I added, before darting upstairs to pack my suitcase.

Don't make this more complicated than it should be! I heard him shout from the kitchen. Please don't. It's not worth it.

Yes, it is, I whispered, imminent tears gathering.

But I managed to hold them back.

63

I boarded the plane to Barcelona and was barely ensconced in my aisle seat when the man next to me started speaking. I recognise you, he said, mentioning my name. I've read your novel and I'm a huge fan. HUGE. I feel like this book was written for me. I relate to everything you say. Your character Charles is basically me. I can't believe I'm meeting you.

I thanked him profusely. Such encounters were rare and tended to remove the few misgivings I occasionally had about writing. There is, after all, no higher compliment than having one's work resonate intimately with a reader. What was the purpose of writing if not to create a conversation between the author, the characters, and the reader? I often stressed that to my students. How novels were a three-way, not a two-way, conversation. The characters were part of that conversation. They led a life of their own. They walked into my books like customers into a shop. I tended to all the customers, but some held more interest than others. The ones who lingered and opened up to me. Soon I knew everything about their past. Where they came from. What they were like as children. What kept them up at night. They became alive. And although I harboured misgivings about Charles, who had so clearly affected my neighbour, it was immaterial. The main thing was that he had become alive for the man who now extended his hand towards mine and shook it vigorously. What more could I ask for?

My name is Juan Tablo, he said. He had a receding hairline, a bristly beard. His stomach protruded slightly from a creased shirt, and there was an unkempt look about him, as if he hadn't changed his clothes in a while.

Juan explained that, although he was born and raised in Spain, he had spent many years in the US, working for a bank. His English sounded American, with a hint of a Spanish accent. He now lived in London, and was on his way to the same literary festival I was speaking at, in Barcelona. He listed a few writers whose talks he was interested in and concluded by saying that I was the one he was most looking forward to hearing. He added that the fact that we were seated next to each other on this particular plane could not be random. It was a sign that we were meant to meet. He believed in signs and clues. In the significance of chance events. And this was one of those events.

Are you married? he asked, as if that too carried some significant meaning. I nodded, then explained that my husband was at home, taking care of our daughter. My husband who made me feel as if I were responsible for most of his ills. Who had called our marriage the biggest mistake of his life. My husband who had not even read the book I was about to discuss at the festival. He resented the two years it had taken me to write it, although he wouldn't admit it. I don't want to be disappointed, he said instead. So I'd rather not read it at all. But I'm happy for you. You know I am.

It was a lame excuse, but I had decided to accept it. Until now. Sitting there, on that plane, it suddenly hit me. He wasn't happy for me. If he hadn't read it, it was because he was afraid that it might be good. And good meant a change in dynamics. A reshuffling of priorities, which neither of us seemed able to tackle. In that sense, we were both as bad as each other. And meanwhile, oblivious to my inner turmoil, Juan Tablo was speaking to me as if we were friends. As if all was well at home and my husband was taking care of our daughter with a loving heart and good intentions, including an adulation of my work, such as Juan was describing it. I *adoolate* your work, he said. But although it was flattering at first, his praise became increasingly irritating. Every time I tried to steer the conversation towards more prosaic matters—literature, London, Juan's job—he would engage for a few minutes before returning to the subject of my book—and Charles. He had no interest in me as a woman, only as a writer. My personality was irrelevant. I was a reader of minds, but only his. It was almost as if he owned me. The way I had brought to life a character that was Juan Tablo's apparent doppelganger meant that something united us. This is what he truly believed. We must have met at some point, he repeated. These occurrences are not happenstance.

I did not mention Charles's limitations to Juan. The fact that my character grappled with his demons and was ultimately unable to confront them. He was, in effect, an akratic and somewhat servile character, though not without charm. I wondered what it was exactly that Juan related to so much, but I refrained from asking. The last thing I wanted to do was encourage further discussion of my novel.

A stewardess appeared with a drinks trolley. Can I get you anything? Juan asked, leaning a little too close to me in the process. His sweat smelled minty.

No thank you.

He settled himself in with a Jack Daniels. I pulled out a yellow pad and explained that it had been a pleasure speaking to him, but that I needed to go over my notes for the talk.

Can I peek? he asked, winking at me.

No, I answered brusquely. Sorry but no.

I looked at my notes. I scribbled in the margin: jerk. Then I quickly crossed it out lest he should see it.

I tried to focus on the conversation I was going to have with the celebrated writer. The key points I wanted to make. I was not entirely prepared. Or perhaps I was, but I still worried it wasn't enough. It was never enough. I was a poor public speaker, always had been. At first being on a stage had paralysed me with fear. These days the paralysis was gone, but the fear remained. Of forgetting what I wanted to say. Of saying the wrong thing. Of stumbling on my words. I was hoping Juan Tablo would leave me in peace. I needed to concentrate. But I could hear him slurping his Jack Daniels next to me. Casting a fleeting glance at my legs. I was wearing a skirt with ankle boots. Now he had pulled the *Economist* magazine out from his bag and was turning the pages loudly, quickly. I wondered whether he was pretending to read. I wished I could change seats. But that would be too rude.

So, I guess you don't really want to speak to me, he began, after a few minutes.

I noticed that he had finished his glass of whisky.

It's not that, I explained gently. It's that I need to go over my notes, as I told you before.

I understand, he said.

A different stewardess came walking down the aisle and he ordered another Jack Daniels.

Well, for what it's worth, here's my story, he said, as if nothing I had just said mattered a jot. As if I wanted to hear his story.

I was married for nine years, no children, he began. Then last summer my wife left me. It wasn't that upsetting, because it was bound to happen. We were no longer getting along. We had nothing in common. She didn't write books like you do. She worked in the perfume industry. She was a good woman, with nice legs and a sense of humour, but not very educated.

And her job was boring. She didn't see it that way, but it was. She loved her colleagues. Always spoke about them. My colleague this, my colleague that. Fuck them all I say. Fuck her colleagues. She never saw things the way I did. Like you, who created Charles, who sees everything like I do.

The stewardess returned with his drink, and he took a few long sips.

Except the bit about the Greek woman, he said, adjusting his seat position. In your novel I mean. I didn't like that bit much. Did I mention that before? I didn't believe he would let himself be seduced by her. But that could be because I don't like Greek people. I would never enter a relationship with a Greek woman. I mean, with another woman, yes, happily, but not a Greek one.

He turned his head back towards me and fixed his gaze in a way that made me understand that I was the other woman he had in mind.

If you want me to stop talking I will, he said.

I explained, yet again, that I needed to go over my notes.

Of course, he said. Apologies.

Now he was making me nervous. I could feel his hungry eyes scanning my body, rather than reading his magazine. I wondered what to do. It clearly hadn't occurred to him that I found him physically repellent. Not only was he convinced that he owned me metaphorically, but now it had become physical.

He finished his whisky and unbuckled his seat belt. He leaned towards me and said he was sorry, he needed to use the toilet. The way he pronounced the word *toilet* was stomach-churning. I could smell the whisky on his breath. As soon as he was gone, I asked the stewardess to move me. It was rude. Insulting. But I could no longer bear being seated next to Juan Tablo.

I was given a seat towards the back of the plane. I tried to hide as I saw him walking past me. At first he didn't notice. But then he stopped and turned round to face me. His eyes were like small, hard pebbles until they eventually softened, veering between pain and disbelief, as if I had betrayed him. He turned away, and walked unsteadily back to his seat, his untucked shirt billowing over his trousers.

I did not see him at my reading. Then again, the event was so crowded I would have been unlikely to spot him.

But I did wonder whether I would have been better off sharing my thoughts rather than moving seats, as I had done. It was rude, and he had probably been hurt. I had clearly crushed his dream about me and my book. It was not every day that a reader identified so intensely with a fictional character. But Juan had been responsible for the crushing.

Later that evening, I went to a fashionable restaurant with the celebrated writer and the organisers of the festival. And there was Juan, sitting a few tables away with a woman. He did not see me at first. But when he did, he lifted his head, looked straight at me, and gave me the middle finger.

64

We had both agreed that Katia would be an only child. Things were difficult enough. Then suddenly I was pregnant, right before Katia's fifth birthday. This surprised me because I was on birth control. Ninety-one per cent effective, I had been told. I stood out as a statistic. A happy statistic. But I was cautious about rejoicing in front of my husband. Another child was not part of the deal.

I'm not sure we'll be able to handle the pressure. Especially after what happened when Katia was born, he reminded me when I finally told him. I can never forget what happened. And there is us too, he added. It might add to the strain.

He was right. It might. Or perhaps it could be heal-ing? Bring us closer together again?

He appeared surprised when I said those words. I thought we were close, he said. When I mentioned the strain, I meant financial. How it affects us. And I'm not ready for another baby.

I could not tell him the truth. That I felt distant from him. How could I not after everything that had happened? Because despite the occasional moments of harmony, everyday life had become difficult. Unpre-dictable. Dark too, in a way I had never anticipated. But I wanted this baby. And I did believe that he or she could work wonders. Restore the light between us. This is what we needed. Light. A new life. Another chance.

This birth will be different from Katia's, I assured him. I know what to expect. I'll take those pills again. And my parents said they'd pay for a nanny. That will make a huge difference. A nanny. And babies bring their own bread. Remember that. And we're doing fine now. Things are better financially. And my father has offered to help a bit with the mortgage.

I don't want another child, he said. I don't want your father's help.

His voice sounded dry, like sand.

I don't want another child.

I won the argument. He could not stop me from hav-ing the baby. Everything was going to be fine. It had to be. I whispered to the unborn child when I could not sleep, which happened often. I hoped my husband was wrong. That her arrival would reduce the stress levels, not increase them. I cradled my stomach once the baby's kicks became stronger. Katia was excited. She wanted to feel the kicks and yelped with joy when she did. But not my husband. Katia insisted and grabbed his hand. Feel the baby, Daddy! Feel it! She pressed his fingers on my stomach and he winced. Do you feel the kicks Daddy? Do you?

Yes, yes, I feel them.

65

Lola arrived one rainy dawn. She flopped out like a ball of wonder, a small kitten. Timid scream, beautiful face, tiny feet. I held her against me and closed my eyes.

My Sweetest, Splendidly Sublime, Sunniest Statistic.

66

We were staying with friends on a Greek island. Lola was a few months old. A beautiful, blue-eyed baby, who slept through the night and gurgled as we wheeled her around the streets of the chora. Whitewashed houses, arcaded courtyards. Men sat at outdoor cafés, smoking and gossiping. Old women in black carried their shopping through narrow alleyways. Sometimes they would stop and fawn over Lola, as did my husband. He was smitten with her. Proud of his daughter's beauty, her temperament, her smile when he beamed at her. He beamed a lot during that time, as did I. Work was going well, he was making money. I spent my days at the beach, alternating between a rocky and a sandy one, with transparent water the likes of which I had never seen before. I could live in a place like this. Divide my days between writing, eating, and swimming. Rent a whitewashed house in one of the crooked alleyways. Sip ouzo in the garden, which smelled of jasmine and lemon blossom. From my terrace I watched a gold-red harvest moon dip slowly into the sea. In the morning, when I awoke, I was alone with my daughters. Strangely, my husband did not exist inside this fantasy.

The day before our departure there was an incident. I was lying on a crowded beach, reading a book while Katia was playing next to me, building a sandcastle. We had gone into the water, the two of us. She had clung onto me, her arms tightly wrapped around my neck. I had tried gently lowering her into the sea, but she resisted. My husband was more persuasive than I was. With him, she let go. But not with me.

Let's build a sandcastle like Leo did! she exclaimed, referring to my friend's son. We walked back to our deck chairs. I dried her vigorously while she jumped up and down. I kissed her wet cheeks. I filled the bucket with sand, then water. We flipped it over together and she squealed with delight as a mini castle emerged. Then she decided she wanted to dig a hole alone. Without you Mummy, she said, sounding proud.

Every couple of minutes I would look up from my book, to be sure she hadn't waded into the sea. I had told her firmly not to.

I should not have taken my eyes off her for a moment, but I did. I was reading *Conjugal Love*, by Alberto Moravia. A rich, newlywed couple has moved to the countryside, where the husband, an egotist and second-rate writer, would like to write a novel. In order to do so, he convinces Leda, his wife, that they must remain abstinent. Leda is upset. There is a barber who comes over every morning to shave the husband's beard—Leda does not trust him.

There was a scream. A woman was pointing at my daughter: she had been knocked down by an incoming swell. A small swell, but enough to terrify Katia. She had walked in without my noticing. I leapt to my feet, ran towards her, and grabbed her out of the water. The woman was very calm. She had noticed Katia before I had, and she was very calm. She looked at me and said something I cannot remember. I was too agitated. We didn't exchange any words because I could not speak. All I could do was shake, just like my daughter was shaking.

It turned out that the woman knew who I was. She was friends with the couple whose house we were staying in. The story was relayed to my husband. It did the rounds. It was spoken about in low voices. I had chosen to read a book while my daughter waded alone in the waves. I tried to defend myself, but there was no defence to be had.

Lousy mother, my husband said. Shame on you. Lousy mother.

❋   ❋   ❋

I had found a stone on that beach. Smooth, ebony black. It glittered in the dark. I carried it around for months, like a talisman.

Its black faded, as did its glitter. Then one day it disappeared. The talisman was dulled. Things got worse again with my husband. It wasn't the stone, of course, but I could not help wondering whether there was some sort of atavistic connection. As if it had registered the shift in the atmosphere.

67

Trouble at work. A disagreement with the CEO, followed by a rift. Now his job was at stake again. I attempted to discuss it. To sound supportive, loving. He looked at me with cold eyes. It's all your fucking fault, he said. All of it. Waste of space. That's what you are. A waste of space.

I began to cry. It happened rarely.

He left the room.

I marked this as the day when my husband ceased entirely to contain himself. Shadows appeared, and their existence took me by surprise. I had never considered myself to be a person of shadows. As the years went by, they became more pronounced.

Swollen shadows.

68

When I think back on the time after Lola turned

three, I remember little. My memories have merged into a blank. A pit of blank. The shadows came down suddenly, like curtains. I recall what I heard. What I felt. What I saw. But not the everyday. Not the humdrum. Only random recollections. As if my neural connections were tampered with. Because there is urgency outside of normality. And that is how I lived for most of that time. In urgency, outside of normality.

I managed to maintain a cool exterior. With writing. Teaching. Taking care of the girls. The occasional lunch or dinner with friends. The truces, too, before his voice rose again—stop, please stop please. Nocturnal card playing. Solitaire. Napoleon at St Helena. Emperor. That cascading shuffle sound, like grinding salt. Empty wine bottles reappeared. But he never seemed drunk. Only slower, angrier, with bilious words spilling from his mouth.

I learned how to walk on eggshells. They were so palpable I could practically see them. Feel them crack under the tips of my toes. How carefully I tried to circumnavigate them. But it happened, every time. And every time it shocked me.

Beneath the shell, the detonation.

The girls were happy. This is what I told myself. They knew nothing, saw nothing. My friends, apart from Julia, knew nothing either. I had always been private that way. I did not want to discuss my marital troubles in public. I did not want others to analyse my situation. I did not want to face their truth. Only mine. I knew their thoughts would make me falter. Falter meant leaving. And for my girls, I could not falter. I could not leave. Not yet. I needed to be as strong as steel. Polished, unbreakable steel.

Waste of space

I can hear their laughs, like bells. Here is Katia, asking Lola and me to join her in her bedroom. She would like us to look at her glass marbles. She pulls a small box out from underneath her bed and displays her new acquisitions. They glow like fluorescent sweets. She names a few. Red devil. Opaque. China. Galaxy. Swirly. Tiger. Cat's eye. Princess. Dragonfly.

They're like swimming colours! Lola exclaims. She leans towards them, and Katia stops her: you can look, but don't touch.

Lola gently places her index finger on the Dragonfly—light green and blue swirls. Wow, she says. And this? She grabs one with multicoloured flecks of glass.

That's the Onionskin, Katia tells her. Put it back, she orders.

She does so reluctantly. Katia closes the box and places it back under her bed. You might want to put that on a shelf instead, I suggest.

Katia hesitates. Maybe later, she says.

Katia's a boy, says Lola. She doesn't like girl things.

Shut up, Katia says.

You're mean, Lola replies, her small face falling.

No fighting allowed. Katia, you must be nice to your sister, I say sternly. Please. Now, would you like to go out to lunch?

Their father isn't home.

I suggest the Italian pizzeria, nearby. Yes! They exclaim.

We leave the house together. We cross the street, holding hands. I can see it. The three of us walking.

Then we turn the corner.

❀   ❀   ❀

My husband returns that night. Katia and Lola tell him about our day. The pizza we ate. The waiter in the restaurant who performed a magic trick for them. How funny he was. And kind.

Their father appears uninterested, distracted. We fight after the girls have gone to bed. A roaring fight.

This time my voice rises louder than his.

How dare you. How dare you speak to me that way. Look at yourself. Look at yourself! You're the nothing, not me. Do you hear? You're the nothing!

He lowers his head. I'm sorry, he says. You're right. I'm sorry. I'm a nothing. Forgive me.

69

In 1953 Jean Giono, the French author, was asked by *Reader's Digest* to write about the most extraordinary person he had ever met.

This is whom he chose and the story he told:

The narrator, a man in his twenties, was hiking through Provence. It was 1913. The landscape was practically barren. He was thirsty and tired. There was barely any trace of civilisation around him, except for derelict buildings. He met a shepherd on the way who offered him a bed for the night. The shepherd, in his fifties, was called Elzéard Bouffier. His wife and only son had both died, and he was a man of few words.

In order to fill the time, Elzéard decided to bring the desolate landscape back to life by cultivating a forest. He showed the narrator the acorns he was planting, one hundred per day. I want to plant one hundred thousand trees, he told him. This is how he stayed happy, and this was his goal. To plant those trees.

The First World War broke out.

The narrator enlisted in the army and did not return to the forest until five years later.

Bouffier was no longer a shepherd—the sheep had been eating the acorns—but a beekeeper. The trees had grown. The once barren landscape was now lush. It was a miracle.

The Second World War broke out, but Bouffier paid no heed. Nothing could stop him planting. The valley was now filled, with new dwellers as well as vegetation. By the time the war ended, Bouffier's trees had brought water, people, and prosperity to the region. The houses, once derelict, had been restored. The area had become an enchanting forest of beech and oaks, and it was soon designated a national park.

Bouffier died of old age, in 1945.

After Giono wrote the story, he revealed that he had actually made it up. Elzéard Bouffier was a figment of his imagination. All over the world, readers were crestfallen. He had to have existed, they argued. Giono wasn't telling the truth.

It felt too real to be made up.

The story resonates deeply with me. It is about transforming sorrow into joy, the barren into the plentiful. About good men planting trees and hope for the world through nature. It is how I want my life to be. How I want everything to be.

I close my eyes.

I am visiting Elzéard's forest. I find comfort in the notion that trees outnumber humans. That they adjust to the slow shift of the seasons with patience and endurance. The majestic beeches and oaks bow to me, tall and vital. The leaves rustle and glow in the dappled sunshine. The branches move slowly, as if dancing. The earth smells of summer rain. I breathe it in deeply. I walk without stopping. I remain there for many hours. A blackbird sings. His serenade echoes through the forest. I am connected. To the bird song, the fragrant earth, the dappled sunshine, the rustling leaves. To the peace surrounding me.

I watch as day becomes dusk becomes night. The sounds are different at night. They belong to nature, not man. But not in my house, where my husband's nocturnal screams shatter the stillness of silence.

70

We are invited to a party in Islington. A literary magazine editor whom I've recently met. I am looking forward to the evening, as many of our friends will be there. But at the last minute my husband changes his mind. I don't want to go, he says. I've got a lot of work to do. I don't care about literary people with their poncy Islington houses.

I'll go on my own then, I tell him. It's important to me. And he doesn't have a poncy house.

I take a bath and get dressed. I ask him to feed the girls. Or perhaps I feed them myself, I don't remember.

Just before leaving the house, he begins to shout. Scream, about something I've done. I am dressed, clasping my handbag, standing by the door, while he continues to scream.

But I have to go, I plead in a shaking voice. I'll be late. Please don't shout. Not now. Please. I'm sorry about whatever it is you're angry about.

He grabs his wallet and shoves me out of the way.

I'm going out, he barks, slamming the door behind him. Look after the children.

The girls are singing in the kitchen because they are happy I stayed home.

My bonnie lies over the ocean, my bonnie lies over the sea, they sing in unison. They do not know that their father has trapped me, like an animal. That he had planned his exit from the start. His shouting was deliberate. He wanted to punish me because this party was important to me. When my friend called, asking where I was, I told her I was unwell. I could feel the lie piercing my vocal cords like a syringe.

❂   ❂   ❂

I take my daughters to visit my parents in Paris. My husband stays behind.

I have a lot of work to do. I'll come next time, he promises.

I know that he won't. He hardly ever visits my parents. Families are not my thing, he says.

They're clearly not, I answer back, remembering too late that such comments carry consequences.

He looks angry. What the fuck does that mean? I want to know. What do you mean by that?

Something jitters inside me.

Nothing. I meant nothing.

❆ ❆ ❆

As soon as she answers the door, my mother declares me too thin. You don't look well, she says.

Later, after the girls have gone to bed, my father makes a disparaging remark. So I shout. The children are in bed, they could not possibly hear me with the door closed. Just as well. I might break something. Anything. I cannot control myself. I am an adult. I shouldn't care so much about what my father says. I should be able to control myself—but I cannot.

Or perhaps this isn't about my father.

I feel the rage mounting. I'm probably going too far, but there is no one else I can shout at. At home I have to be strong. But with my parents I can be weak. And I need to shout. I need to be weak. I need to rage and break and cry. I haven't in a long time.

So I do. At my father, my mother. I am child again, no longer a wife or a mother. A screaming child who's forgotten why it even started, only that it had to come out.

I hear the sound of small feet. Suddenly the girls are there, standing in the doorway, staring at me.

71

The Jardin du Luxembourg.

I buy my daughters pink candyfloss and we sit in an outside café, underneath a chestnut tree. We visit the merry-go-round, where Lola waves at me from atop a wooden horse. I take them to the playground and sit with Lola on a rusty green cast-iron chair while

Katia tackles the climbing frame. Children laugh and shriek all around us. Then Lola says she would like to go on the swing. She settles herself on the seat and I push her high into the air. She squeals with delight. She is happy. So is Katia.

Now Lola would like to ride the train. The wooden one with the yellow doors.

I lift her into the train and place her on a seat. She pretends to sound an invisible horn. *Beepbeepbeep!* she cries out. I hear my phone ring. It must be my mother. I pick it up and speak quickly. Yes, I'll buy some bread on the way home, and milk too. A child calls for his mother and I think it is Katia. But no, it isn't. She is still playing by the climbing frame, this time with a boy.

I replace the phone in my bag, and, when I look up again, Lola is no longer sitting on the train.

Lola? I call out. But there is no answer. In her place sits a little boy wearing glasses.

Have you seen the little girl who was sitting here before you? I ask him, trying to sound calm. Blonde hair, blue eyes?

He shakes his head and answers in a language I cannot recognise.

I can feel the colour vanish from my cheeks, the throb inside my throat.

I can barely breathe as I start looking for Lola, frantically calling her name, stopping a few small girls who look like her from afar but are not her. A couple walks over towards me. Americans. The woman is holding a sleeping baby in her arms. He has a slipper missing. Hey don't worry, the woman says. Your daughter can't be far. And security won't let her out alone.

But where is security? I cry out. I don't see security, do you? I point towards the main entrance, where a lone man sits behind a till, surrounded by sweets and plastic toys.

I think the security guy is usually inside the play-ground, the woman answers, gently bouncing her baby, who is making small noises. Or maybe he's not here today. But it's cool, and you shouldn't worry, she adds. You'll find your daughter, of course you will.

I am trembling now. I don't know, I say. I really don't know if it's cool.

The couple look at me strangely. We think you'll be fine. She's like, gotta be here, right? But hey, good luck. Take care.

Something awful has happened to my daughter. I can feel it in my bones. She could easily have walked out of here with a total stranger. Lola trusts everybody. I can picture her slipping her hand into an unfamiliar one, a man with calloused fingertips. The thought makes me want to retch. The more I think about it, the more detailed the scenario becomes. I can see the man and his fingers. His teeth are rotten. His insides are aflame. I know I'm overreacting. But it is beyond me. I am aware of my fear, as brittle as winter twigs, aware of the fact that several people are staring at me as I begin to circle the playground like a mad-woman, clutching my handbag against me, step after step after step. A few other parents offer to help, but I don't respond. An African woman with a patterned orange dress tries to reassure me. Her voice is deep and pleasant, like a bass instrument. I will find your daughter, she tells me. Don't worry, she can't be far. I will help you.

Now Katia has sidled over to me with a worried expression, parched lips.

Where is Lola? she asks, grabbing my hand.

I look at Katia and see her big father in the shape of her small face. The slant of her blue-grey eyes. I have always been aware of the resemblance between them, now even more so. Except that, unlike her father, my daughter is soft like velvet. She is nervous, I can tell. Her lips are always parched when she's nervous. But I don't have it in me to reassure her. I cannot be a mother. My heart is beating too fast. I am a frantic, terrified child-woman who has lost her daughter. I have no control over my own motherhood. I have no more authority. It is gone. I have no dominion over myself. This is the truth. And this is why my husband takes advantage of me.

And then I hear a cry. The African woman has found her, by the seesaw. Here she is, the woman smiles. Here is your little one. She has been calling for you.

Lola is smiling, utterly unaware of what I have just gone through. I break down as I hug her tightly against me. I turn around to thank the African woman, but she is gone. I catch a glimpse of her orange dress as she exits the playground, a small boy in tow. Thank you, I whisper.

Lola is babbling now, telling me that she walked to the seesaw on her own, like a big girl. Look, look at the ducks, she says, pointing at the seesaw in question. I wanted to sit on the ducks.

I see no ducks, only a giraffe painted on wood. But I don't care, because she is there, alive, my angel, my daughter. I cannot stop hugging her, and after a while she gently pushes me away. I want a lollipop, she says.

I am not sure how long the whole incident lasted. It could have been an hour, or a few minutes. And this is what strikes me most. How the world stopped, and how I felt myself inching closer to somewhere between despair and insanity. I think Katia felt it too. That somehow her beloved mother was teetering on the edge of something indistinct, like dark, shadowed water.

72

The peregrine falcon is the fastest bird on earth. The golden eagle is a competitor, followed by the white-throated needletail, the Eurasian hobby, the frigate bird, and the gyrfalcon. Albatrosses and common swifts do not lag far behind.

Mine is the flight of the white-throated needletail. Its breeding ground covers Central Asia, Southern

Siberia, Southern Asia, and the Indian subcontinent. I take off, my daughters hanging on.

Where are we going? they ask.

Far, I answer. Very far. Where I can live untied.

73

I have left my daughters in the care of my parents for a few days. I am going to visit my friend Paola in Genoa, where she now lives. I plan on spending a night with her before going to Rome, to stay with my sister.

Of all my friends from my younger years, the only ones I've regularly kept in touch with are Nadine, who lives with her family in Germany, and Paola. That bright, spirited, and fiercely ambitious woman is now a highly regarded scientist. But her dreams of marriage and children were never fulfilled. When she last visited me, shortly after Lola was born, there was a sadness in her eyes. The sadness was also reflected in the weight she had gained, in the unattractive brash blonde of her hair. But this time, as she opens the door, I can immediately tell that something has changed. She has lost weight, and her hair is back to its original colour. As she walks me through her sparsely furnished but tasteful apartment—colourful stones dotted around the room, black and white photographs hanging on the walls—she speaks quickly and excitedly. It transpires that Paola has recently fallen in love with a widower, whose wife died of cancer a couple of years back. The man in question, S., is a geologist and a bit eccentric. His obsession is minerals, and his living room is filled with them. As a matter of fact, Paola says, his house looks like a museum. Stones fill every shelf and space: Chlorargyrite. Granite. Chrysolite. Amethyst. Quartz. Rhodisite. Blue spinel. Stibiconite. Pyrite. Paola knows their names by heart, she announces, with barely dissimulated pride, pointing towards her own small collection. It's contagious, she says. I suspect I'll have to build new shelves soon.

I mention Katia and her love of marbles. I describe how she plays and the care with which she looks after them. But she's a child, and they're obviously not as valuable as these, I add, glancing towards Paola's shelf. Some of the stones glow in the early evening light.

Paola answers that hers are not particularly valuable, unlike S's. The oldest one in his collection is an obsidian. He thinks it might be Aztec, from the fifteenth century. Obsidian is sharp. Razor sharp. The Aztecs used it for weaponry. Axes. Knives. It was also considered divine and had medicinal properties. A good physician, according to the Aztecs, was one who had knowledge of herbs, roots, and stones. I find that fascinating, Paola tells me. Maybe we scientists should look into that again: herbs, roots, and stones.

A whole new world has opened for me, she smiles. As it did for S. when he first discovered it. He admitted that he had never thought an inanimate object could touch him that way, could revive his spirits as it did, especially after his wife's death. Those minerals have provided him with an unexpected solace. As has Paola.

I mention the stone I found on the Greek beach. The way its surface changed with the years. I also felt as if it had powers. Not divine but magical. But perhaps that was a projection. Perhaps all magic is a projection.

Yes, as a scientist I would tend to agree, Paola replies. But that doesn't mean that it must be dismissed. The fact is that the connections between rituals and mankind are important. Ancient. We might not all believe that magic is statistically real, but we cannot deny that it has power. And power is an incontrovertible fact. It lives everywhere.

74

Later that evening, Paola and I share a bottle of wine and pasta al pesto in one of Genoa's best osterias.

Paola tells me more about S. She met him at a conference. At first he didn't seem that interested in her, but then, after they had gone out together a few times, she realised that he was infatuated—and so was she. We've barely been apart at all. Actually, tonight is the first time! Paola laughs. She has wide lips with small teeth. There is something childlike about her. I cannot remember whether she was that way when I first knew her. After all, we were both still young at the time. I did not pay attention to such things. I took life for granted, including the fact that Paola's desire to settle down clashed with my vision of a successful career. Of one who would dictate her own terms in life. This is what I wish I had told my now-deceased uncle. That when I was younger, I truly believed I would have control over my destiny. Nothing would interfere with my plans, because I held the power.

This was before I met my husband and understood that my vision of power was entirely skewed. It might have lived everywhere, as Paola stated, but it was out of reach when I needed it. Because life had not turned out as I expected. It was as fragile as lace. It dissolved between my fingers. In my heart. No terms could be dictated. Whatever I ended up with would always be instead of something else.

75

A waiter refills our glasses. Paola is telling me about S. He's a bit eccentric, she repeats. But I love him. She shows me a picture of him on her phone. That's him, she says. And he's a very good lover by the way. He's had many women in his life.

What I see is a stocky man with a vibrant face. I mention the vibrancy. I don't comment on his many lovers.

I like the look of him, I say. I'm very happy for you.

Thank you.

She takes a sip of her wine and then looks at me. She says that I seem a bit different. Harder, she says. The word shakes me: harder. Why would she say that?

Is everything all right? she asks. How's work?

I answer that it's fine, wondering again what she means by harder. I still teach at the same university, twice a week. Sometimes I get fed up with it, but that's normal. And the salary is good.

OK. And family life? Your husband? I'm talking and talking, and I've barely asked you anything about him. I only met him a couple of times, she adds. I can't say I know him well.

I tell her that my husband works long hours. His pay is low, and he's looking for a new job. He's had many in the last ten years. I don't tell her that, at first, I had assumed that it was the jobs he picked that were the problem, not him. But now I know better. I wonder increasingly about him, and his state of mind. When he isn't working he plays video games, which have replaced cards. And he drinks, even more than he used to. He is careful to get rid of the bottles before I can count them, but I suspect that at least one a night is consumed. I watch him from afar. The way he pours the wine. The way he holds his glass. The way his eyes focus on the games when he plays, moving the joystick with intense concentration. I tried to address his nightly habits several times, but it came to nothing, apart from him asking me to mind my own business. Shouting when I tried to take it further. Therefore, this is how we live, the two of us. Each one of us in their own corner, minding their own business, their own unhappiness. Often in the morning he tries to pretend that everything is normal. But it is a sham, and we both know it. We are gradually drifting apart. He has become detached, sullen. When he speaks to me it is about practicalities or the girls. They are the one thing that binds us. They are his everything, as he often reminds me. They are my everything too, but I don't feel the need to formulate it as such. It is a given. I live my children, my work. But I do not live my husband anymore. I have come to realise that he was only ever a man I thought could fill the hole which love had left empty. The hole left by Alexander.

Family life is all right, I say to Paola. Nothing major. Just the usual ups and downs.

Then I admit that what I'd really like to discuss is my second novel, rather than my husband. It is to be published next spring, and I'm looking forward to it coming out. For a long time I was grappling with my writing, unable to find inspiration—and then I did. I had been staring at it all along, without realising that my own story was the answer.

This has the intended effect, and Paola urges me to tell her more.

I explain that my book is about a young man who disappears. It is inspired by something that happened to me, a story I have shared with very few people. Not even my own sister. But with Paola I'm in safe waters. I can feel it.

I recount my encounters with Alexander when I was sixteen. How they lasted a total of two hours and had a profound effect on my life. How I fell in love with him immediately. As if I had found a missing person I had been searching for without realising it. How I still thought about him even though it was so many years ago.

When I am done speaking Paola looks at me. She finds the story tragic, especially how I found Alexander slumped against that squat door. She asks if I ever went looking for him, and I shake my head. I didn't know how or where to start, I tell her. And perhaps part of me is afraid of seeing him again, I add.

I've never expressed this truth before, and it startles me.

Paola leans back against her chair. Yes, she says. You're afraid that he might not live up to the expectations you have of him. You only met him for two hours after all. That's not enough time to get to know a person. I suspect he's very different from what you remember. He's suffered, after all. And people change when they suffer.

Yes. Alexander is probably an entirely different man today, not one I might relate to at all. But the certainty of that moment in 1985 has never left me. There is no doubt in my mind that at the time he felt the same way. He might not anymore, but he did. I could see it in his sixteen-year-old eyes. And I'm pretty sure he has never forgotten me. I'm intrinsically tied to one of the most devastating episodes of his life. Such things can never be forgotten. It marked me. He marked me. Which is why I've written this book.

It's very understandable, says Paola. His mother's death interrupted the bloom and the promise of a possible love between you. You were reminded of that when you saw him again. And that is terribly painful.

Yes. She is right. The bloom and the promise of a possible love.

A promise cut short never goes away, she continues. That's why your feelings for him are so powerful. But it doesn't mean they're reliable.

I look at her. What do you mean?

It means that you might be disappointed if you see him again. As I said before, people change when they suffer, and not always for the better.

I know that, I reply. But it doesn't stop me wondering how he's turned out. Who he's become. I'd like to see for myself.

Paola takes another sip of her wine. OK. What happens in your book. Does your character ever see him again?

She travels the world, but never does, no.

And in real life? What do you think is going to happen? I mean, if you really wanted to, you could find him, *non credi*? Don't you think?

Yes. Maybe. Yes.

She raises her eyes and looks at me, but says nothing.

The following day I visit the Palazzo Rosso Museum. Paola is teaching that morning. I was up all night, unable to sleep. I thought back on everything she had said. The promise cut short. The fact that he might be a different man today. That I might be disappointed. That I never went looking for him. It is an important question: why didn't I? Could I now, if I wanted to? No, I couldn't. My thoughts will need to be clear, unobstructed, if I am to go looking for Alexander. And nothing is clear at home. I live on a permanent high wire. A high wire with occasional moments of reprieve. And for those moments, I have chosen to stay. But for how long?

At 6.00 a.m. I searched online for the Dante poem Akhmatova had written. The one I had first read in Alexander's book.

> He did not return, even after his death, to
> That ancient city he was rooted in.
> Going away, he did not pause for breath
> Nor look back. My song is for him.
>
> I whisper it to myself.
> My song is for him.

In the museum I stand in front of a Van Dyck portrait of a noble Genoese family: Geronima Brignole-Sale and her daughter, Maria Aurelia.

The pose is stiff, the fabric lush. A red drape hangs in the background. Geronima is dressed in a long black velvet dress. The sleeves have soft white cuffs, like veils. Her high collar, of the same white, looks cumbersome. Her face is both haughty and sad. Maria Aurelia stands by her mother, her white satin and brown dress as regal as Geronima's.

How old is she? I wonder. Seven, possibly eight. I look at their faces, mother and daughter. There is something impenetrable about them. How was life at home, in 1627? Was Geronima's husband good to his wife? Did he love her unconditionally or did he demean her? And, if so, did she fight back?

I feel like reaching out and touching the canvas.

The velvet of her dress. The tip of her slender, white fingers.

Tell me, I whisper to Geronima. Tell me what it was like for you.

Let me touch the tip of your slender, white finger.

Let me touch time gone.

❁   ❁   ❁

My husband calls me later that day.

I just wanted to say that I'm sorry. About the things I said to you, in the last year or so. The horrible things, I mean. I don't really mean them, he adds, sounding contrite.

So I'm not a waste of space then? The biggest mistake of your life?

No, you're not. Of course you're not.

So why do you say such hurtful things to me then?

He clears his throat before speaking. Why do I say them? Because I'm under pressure, that's why. Work has been a fucking nightmare, can't you see that? Can't you accept my apology, rather than use it as an opportunity to attack me? Don't you think that would be a better tactic?

I'm not attacking you. I'm just asking.

Yes, you're attacking me. You often do, without knowing it. You just blurt things out without thinking.

His tone has hardened now, and I know better than to respond.

OK.

That's it? OK?

Yes. And thank you for your apology.

Yeah right, he says, before slamming the phone down.

In Rome my sister takes me up four flights of stairs to a large, sunlit penthouse flat on the Via Margutta. She is here on a research grant, and the accommodation has been provided by the French Academy. We're very lucky, she says. Not in my wildest dreams did I think I'd nab a flat like this.

As I stand on the terrace she points out the sprawling views of the city, stretching from the church of Trinità dei Monti across the Tiber river all the way to St Peter's Basilica. To the ochre-coloured city walls, the wide expanse of sky.

If I could, I would live here too. Drink in the beauty. Live a leisurely life—two words which, over the years, have increasingly become a contradiction in terms.

I think of my husband's phone call and his words, *can't you accept my apology*? In fact I cannot accept it, because it has come too late. His apology has become meaningless. It would have meant everything not so long ago.

But now it leaves me cold.

❊   ❊   ❊

My sister has cut her auburn hair short. Over lunch on her penthouse terrace, her blue eyes peer at me from her freckled face. Like mine, her eyes are outlined by dark, thick lashes, giving the impression that she is permanently made-up. A blessing, my mother has often commented. You girls have my father to thank for this.

I also share her father's tall and slender body, while my sister is a few inches shorter. And unlike hers, my hair is dark and wavy. I often wear it up in a smooth bun, as is the case today.

Would you like a tour of the city? she asks, filling our glasses with water. A slice of lemon bobs inside the jug.

A friend of hers, Mauro, knows Rome like no one else. He'd be happy to show you around, she tells me. He owes me a translation, she adds.

My sister teaches French at La Sapienza, the local university. She also writes books about literary theory which I find slightly impenetrable. Her fiancé, O., is an American academic who's a specialist in Russian literature. There is something quiet and steady about their relationship which I envy. They speak in low voices and apparently hardly ever fight. I'm not sure whether this is good or bad. But the point is that she's happy. So happy that they do everything together, she tells me, over a pungently dressed endive salad. Shopping, eating, travelling, reading, jogging. We've never been apart for more than three days. We even think together, she jokes, dipping a piece of bread into the dressing.

To me this is anathema. Notwithstanding the tension in my marriage, I cannot see how doing everything all the time with anyone is a good thing. I need time alone. To reflect. Recharge. Take a deep breath. If I didn't, I would not be able to function properly. Not even with my daughters would I contemplate doing everything, however much I love them. In fact, more than once I have found myself bored by their company. Wishing I was elsewhere. Writing my book, for instance. Or walking the streets quickly. I like to walk quickly. A couple of times, in London, I went to the cinema alone, just as I had done as a teenager. The soft, crackling sound of the opening screen hadn't lost any of its appeal. Coming out of that darkened room into the glare of day provoked that same delicious *frisson* of misbehaviour. I had sought to replicate it with my daughters, but somehow children's films did not have the same effect. Did that say something about me? Or was boredom one of the inescapable factors of motherhood? I still don't know the answer. And even if I did, I would not share it with my sister, who is expecting her first child. She is four months pregnant and shows me her latest ultrasound scan. The grainy image of a small baby. It's so exciting, she says. Do you remember getting ultrasounds? she asks. I do. Very well. I remember that same trepidation. Looking forward to meeting the baby in the grainy picture. Choosing a name, buying the clothes. Except that in my case motherhood was something I had to learn, rather than ease into naturally. I do not need to remind my sister of what happened after I gave birth to Katia. She does not need reminding. Not at this stage. She has waited long enough for this child, and chances are her experience will be significantly different from mine. Easier. She's an older mother. A natural mother.

She brings an apple cake to the table and we both pick at it quietly.

I've been thinking about what happened when Katia was born, she says, as if reading my thoughts. You called me during that time, and I wasn't there for you.

It's fine, I tell her, surprised to hear her mention it. It was a long time ago. And we've talked about it before.

Yes. But I don't think I quite grasped what you must have gone through. And now that I'm expecting my first child, I do.

I look at her gently. Thank you. But it won't happen to you. I'm sure it won't. And I think about it too, I add. But, as I said, it was a long time ago.

I'm not worried about it happening to me, she answers. I'm only saying I should have been more understanding.

My sister was in Dakar, working as an aide to the married French cultural attaché, with whom she was conducting a torrid affair. He was thinking of leaving his wife. They conducted their affair in her apartment. That was when my mother rang and told my sister she needed to get on the next plane to London. It seemed I was very unwell.

I didn't want to leave, to tell you the truth, my sister admits. I was having the time of my life. I didn't really care about my sister's sleep deprivation. That's all I thought it was. Sorry, but true, she adds. I was young, selfish, and in love with the attaché who was clearly never going to leave his wife. But at the time I didn't know it and was enjoying my moment in the sun. Literally.

I smile. Fair enough.

I only realised how serious it was when I saw you, she says. It freaked me out.

I nod. But, in fact, I do not remember seeing her. I remember little of those few days, apart from the smell of the starchy white sheets in the hospital room.

Nothing else.

78

A few hours after Katia's birth, a nurse came in and asked me to sign a document. In the section 'mother' I wrote my mother's name. The nurse looked confused. I rectified it, embarrassed. *I* was the mother.

MOTHER. Slow mother. I felt the love but found it hard to let it flow.

I was not prepared. For her permanent cries. For the painful breastfeeding. For the exhaustion that invaded my body like fog. For that loose wire, disconnecting inside me. I felt as if my head had become colonised by a nest of ants.

79

I dropped her. I was holding her upright when suddenly I was not. When I came to, I found her on the ground, screaming.

And again, every day from then on.

I dropped her from her changing table. Walking from one room to the next. While I was standing. Speaking on the phone. At night, in bed. When I was simply looking at her.

Drop.
Drop.
Blackout.

80

I had read about postnatal depression, but I was unable to make the connection between what I had read and what I was experiencing. I didn't consider myself to be someone who fell into a category. Categories belonged to others, not me. I had always lived outside conventions, as had my parents. None of this could be applied to me. Therefore, there was no point in sharing this with anyone, not even my husband.

A form of narcissism, perhaps? Self-delusion?

Or perhaps delusion is simply a form of narcissism.

My husband witnessed a blackout. I was feeding Katia when, according to him, I suddenly went silent and strange. Like, your eyes looked really weird, he said. Your eyelashes fluttered.

I spoke calmly. I did not mention that I had dropped our daughter on several occasions because I did not want to alarm him. But I did admit to losing consciousness a few times. That when it happened it felt as if I had just returned from somewhere very far away. Like a seizure.

My husband could not handle the concepts of 'far away' or seizures of any kind. Not in his mother, and certainly not in his wife.

It will pass, he said. You're just tired, that's all.

Maybe.

I'm sure it will pass, he repeated. But if it doesn't then we'll decide what to do.

It continued to happen. But no decisions were made.

A health visitor came to the house. I mentioned how my daughter never slept. Her cries, night and day. My difficulties with breastfeeding.

I think she has colic, the health visitor said, before giving me a few tips.

She asked how I was feeling. Was anyone giving me a hand? My husband, for example?

Sometimes he does, I said. But it's hard to wake him up at night. So it's mostly me. But I'm coping. I'm fine. Just a bit shattered, that's all.

81

I had taken Katia in her brand-new pushchair to the nearby park. It was a beautiful spring day. I had had another sleepless night, and I remember feeling it so acutely that I feared I might be the one falling to the ground this time, not her. But I wanted her to get some air. And it would do me good too, I reasoned.

I arrived in the park and circled it a few times. There were other mothers doing the same thing. Going nowhere in particular. Circling the park, pushing a pram. Some mothers were with friends or partners, others on their own. But there was a communal solitude between us. That is how I saw it. And that communal solitude made me feel better.

I sat down on a bench, beside an oak tree. I had forgotten to bring a bottle of water and I was thirsty. Increasingly thirsty. I got up and my head spun. I needed to find a café or shop where I could buy water. I saw one in the distance, no more than two or three minutes away. Its awning was red and white. Maybe I could leave Katia alone while I went to the red and white shop. After all, she was peacefully asleep. There was no point in moving the pram if she was sleeping. The last thing I wanted to hear was her piercing wails. I had read that babies' cries increased oxytocin levels and brought a mother closer to her child. But this did not apply to me. It pushed me further away. Because, no matter how much I tried to comfort her, Katia did not stop crying. Sometimes it could go on for hours at a time. Mosquito cries. They buzzed in my ear, penetrating my whole being. Katia mosquito. I could not swat the cries away. I had to endure them. And then there was the breastfeeding. I held my daughter against me, burped and breastfed her, because that was the thing to do. But I hated it. She tugged at my nipples and the ensuing rush often made me feel faint. I realised that it triggered the seizures. That, if I stopped, they might go away. But I could not stop because breastfeeding was vital, especially during the first three months. This is what I had been told. So I gave in. I wanted my daughter to thrive. My vital Katia.

But now she was quiet, content. She slept soundly, clenching her little fists by her head. She was beautiful and peaceful. I could not risk moving her. She would wake up if I did. I just knew it.

I left Katia in her pram and walked to the other side of the park, where I had spotted that café—just there, not even three minutes away. Except that, as I walked, it started to feel further than I had thought—but, then again, my whole notion of time had been skewed.

I found myself overcome by an enormous feeling of peace. Of relief. I was walking alone in the park. My beautiful new-born baby was sleeping, and I was walking alone. There was a smell of something sweet in the air, like honey, and I inhaled it deeply. Blissfully.

As I approached the café, I slowly became aware that what I was doing was probably not a good idea. That a person could snatch Katia and walk away with her. Or that someone could spot the pram with the baby minus her mother and call the police. I turned round. I could see the pram just where I had left it, beside the oak tree. There was no crying. No noise at all. No one in Katia's vicinity. All was well.

I walked on. I reached the café and bought a bottle of water. I drank it quickly and dabbed some water on my wrists, my temples. I was still feeling a little dizzy and I thought that might help. When it didn't, I sat down again on a nearby chair. Just for a minute, I remember thinking to myself. A minute before heading back to my baby.

I took a few deep breaths, then closed my eyes. I do not remember what happened afterwards, only that I woke up with a sudden jolt, to the sound of a barking dog. I rushed back towards the pram, and from afar saw that, in my absence, a crowd had gathered around that oak tree. Katia was screaming now, and a woman was holding her upright. A woman whom I did not know was holding my baby daughter. Others were speaking heatedly, and a man was making a phone call. I started running. All symptoms of dizziness had disappeared. I ran like I had never run before. I arrived breathless, sweat pouring down my face, my heart beating against my shirt. This is my daughter! I shouted at the women around me. Get away from her!

I wrenched Katia away from the woman's arms— her face was taut and angry: do you realise your baby has been left unattended for twenty minutes? Screaming alone in her pram, without her mother by her side? How could you leave a baby alone like that? Is something wrong with you! And we've called the police. You can explain it to them. I'm sure they'll know what to do.

Twenty minutes? That wasn't possible. Had I really been gone that long? And was something wrong with me? Possibly so. But what was it? What had happened to me? If it hadn't been for that dog, I might have slept for much longer. And possibly returned to an empty pram. The thought was inconceivable, and I felt a wave of nausea overtake me. I placed a crying Katia back in her pram, which is when the police arrived. I managed to explain, over her cries and with a faltering voice, that I had gone to buy some water. That I hadn't realised how far it was. That my baby had kept me up all night and that I had worried she would wake up if I moved her. So I had left her there, under the tree. I did not admit that I had closed my eyes and fallen momentarily asleep. I did not admit it because I understood that what I was saying sounded abnormal. Mothers did not leave their babies alone—and I had. The policewoman was now looking at me with some concern, as if I were ill and required attention.

Someone rang my husband. Your wife is not well, the person said. Your wife is not well.

The sound of those five words. I had never been not well before. And, as if further proof were required, I vomited before having another blackout, in front of the policewoman. I ended up in hospital for a few days. A severe form of postpartum depression was diagnosed. That was when my sister and parents came to see me. But I was drugged up. I only vaguely remember the outline of faces, drifting in out and of focus.

My husband's was not one of them.

82

The woman from social services came to visit me in hospital. She wore glasses which covered the upper half of her face. I remember focusing on the lower half. Her mouth as it moved, the feral words that flew from her painted lips. I was not in a fit state to look after my daughter, she said. I had left her alone and walked away.

Therefore I'm sorry but—

Therefore I'm sorry but—

I drowned her last words. I might even have covered my ears to drown them better.

They were going to take my baby away.

83

There was a doctor I vaguely remember. Then waking up, a few days later, in my own bed.

I could not recall how I had got there. All I knew

was that my baby had been taken away from me. I was not fit to be a mother. I would never know the joy, the love, because I had jeopardized my only chance. My mind had derailed, and I had lost control. All I wanted to do was go back to sleep and never wake up. There was no point in living anymore. None. Except that my mother was standing beside me, saying something. It seemed I was speaking out loud. But darling, Katia is with us! No one is taking her away. They think the postpartum also includes some sort of temporary epilepsy, which was triggered by the exhaustion. That's why you had blackouts.

Epilepsy?

Yes. No more breastfeeding either. She's on the bottle now. You need to take pills for a while, and everything will be fine. You have nothing to fear anymore. Nothing.

I sat up quickly, and my head began to spin. Where is she? Can I see her? I need to see her.

Her smell. Her sound. Her being.

Not right now, my mother said gently. But I'll bring her in later today.

84

My parents looked after Katia, with the help of a nanny. We need you to be strong again, they kept repeating.

I knew that Social Services was behind those words. That everyone was keeping a close eye on me, including my husband. He was incandescent about what had happened. Although he initially tried to express some sympathy, I could sense his unease.

It was hard for him to admit that his own wife had been on the brink of insanity. That he had seen nothing coming. And that it might happen again. This was his fear. That it might happen again.

Social workers made a few more visits until Katia turned one. The woman with the large glasses was one of them. During her last visit, when Katia was eight months old, the two of us had a cup of tea together. She told me that in her spare time she wrote poetry. Her partner Mike thought she was rather good.

85

Guilt and shame. For years they traipsed heavily in my shadow. I had thought I would be a perfect mother. Instead, I had failed my daughter. And I had nearly lost her. I can still see her smile when the two of us were finally reunited. The way her tiny hand touched my cheek.

It breaks my heart. Every time.

My sister is speaking about the incident. She wants me to know that although she wasn't there for me, my parents and friends were. I could have reached out, explained that I was feeling exhausted, unable to cope, but I chose to say nothing.

I was not in a state of mind to make choices, I reply. I was not my normal self at all.

And somewhere in the back of my mind was the knowledge that my proximity to madness might drive my husband away. When I had finally told him about it, he had reacted badly. He had lived through it once, with his mother. He could not live through it again, with his wife. So I chose to say nothing after that.

My sister shakes her head slowly. Ventures that perhaps my husband is the one with a problem, not me. What sort of husband doesn't stand by his wife? I mean, what a selfish jerk. And it's not like you were mad, but ill, she says. There's a big difference there, wouldn't you agree?

Yes, I would.

Which brings her to the crux of the matter. She doesn't know about my life at home because I hardly ever discuss it. With her, my sister, she says. With our parents. You keep all the heavy shit in and then we get the leftovers. What's going on with your strange husband?

My strange husband. She has never used those words before, and I flinch. He is more than strange. He is volatile, unpredictable, abusive. At least he used to be. Now we barely speak to each other. He has become an enigma to me. A puzzle. One neither he nor I can seemingly solve. But I cannot tell her that, because I've never liked discussing my marital life with my family. My children, certainly, but not their father. My parents have always been discreet about him, but not my sister. For years she has pried, with few results. But now my resistance is starting to crumble, like chalk.

It's always been like that with you, my sister is saying. Not the episode with Katia, that was different. Obviously different. But, in general, we always get the leftovers without knowing where they're coming from. As I said, it's heavy.

I don't know. Maybe.

But it's true. Mum thinks so too. She's afraid to bring stuff up because she thinks you'll get upset. I feel the same, by the way. It's hard to talk to you. Like it is now. You're defensive.

No, I'm not. What do you want to talk about?

My sister takes a sip of water and carefully sets the glass back on the table. Sometimes there's a real need for outside assistance, she says, looking straight at me. For family. You can't always rely on yourself. There're some things we can't navigate alone. Personally, I've never minded outside assistance. I like reaching out to my friends. And to my sister.
  I'm glad. And?
  She is getting under my skin. That old, familiar impatience creeping in.

And I want to know how things are going at home. Are you happy? You don't look happy. We're all a bit worried about you.

Are you? Well I don't know. It's hard to know when one is happy.

No, it's not. I'm happy. Not hard to tell.

OK, well that's great.

Yes, it is, my sister replies, undeterred. I have another question then. Are you still in love with your husband?

This takes me by surprise, and I pause before answering.

I don't know. I was when we first met.

And now? What do you feel now?

I don't know, I mutter.

What happened? Did anything happen?

I hesitate: a few things.

She sighs loudly. Here we go again. I don't know. A few things. Maybe.

Don't say anything to your sister, for god's sake. Keep it all to yourself until you fucking explode. Just keep it in forever.

She has caught me off guard. It's not like that, I tell her. It's really not like that.

Yes, it is, she answers. It really is.

86

As far as I can recall, my sister has never lived alone. There was always a boyfriend or a roommate in the picture. After she met O. their Bastille flat in Paris became a stopover for countless friends and lodgers.

Mauro's cousin was one of them until he found his own accommodation, she explains. His cousin's a nice guy. But Mauro's the special one. And very good looking, she adds. He and his wife are both classical musicians, she adds. Really talented.

I help my sister clear the table. I've got a class to teach, she tells me as I dry the dishes. Do you want me to ask Mauro if he's free?

No, it's OK. I'd rather walk around alone.

And that's when I choose to tell her about my marriage. When she's putting the dishes away and there is little time left for discussion. What I say requires few words, no discussion. I speak quickly and breathlessly. I conclude by saying that the situation at home is not good at all. In fact, it's getting worse by the day—and my husband is not the only culprit. I've become a resentful woman. I've let it seep into my system. I provoke him. It is my only defence against him. We are both losers in this war. I should never have married him. My only blessings are my daughters.

My sister looks at me in disbelief, holding the same plate she has been holding since I started to speak.

Jesus, Clara, that's pretty bad. I don't know what to say. I'm very sorry to hear it. How do you function?

I don't know. I just do. But there's little peace. No possibility of a truce. Not at this stage. But I still manage to work, despite it all, I add. Writing is my only solace, apart from my children.

My sister places the plate in a wooden rack and turns round to face me.

I'm very glad you've told me. But you've chosen to do so at the worst time, when I have to run to a class. You did it on purpose. I can see that. Can we talk about this later? I really want to.

I shake my head and explain that I would rather not. There's not much to talk about. It is what it is. Whatever happens next is for me to decide, not him. The only certainty I have is that this cannot go on. I cannot live like this anymore. It is slowly dismantling me.

My sister leans towards me and squeezes my hand. I sort of figured that was the case. And I'm here for you. Just know that.

Thank you.

She looks at me. You must leave him. Not only for

you, but for your daughters. They cannot live like this. It will dismantle them too in the end.

87

It is a warm day, and the sun, the colour of saffron, is high. I amble through the back streets of the *centro*. Past barbers, booksellers and butchers, antique shops with golden lettering, a pharmacy with apothecary bottles in its windows. In a nearby bar a group of old men, their skin crinkled like winter leaves, play cards in silence. There is much to be inspired by: the cobblestones I tread and the colour of the Roman stone. The faces I encounter: nubile women with big dark eyes and skimpy clothing, a small girl with her mother. Couples holding hands, gnarled old men like those in the bar. I pass fountains with sea horses and tritons cast in marble as white as sugar. Palazzos with majestic carvings, ochre walls, and intricate ironwork. I stop at the Pantheon and gaze at its large, ancient dome. Later I grab one of the remaining tables in a café and order an espresso. By speaking to my sister, a weight has been lifted off my shoulders. A greater weight than I had imagined. Until now, Julia's support had been paramount. But she is not my sister. There are some things she would not dare say. *You must leave him* is one of them. Only my sister could say that without appearing to overstep the boundaries. She is right to be upset. I should have trusted her from the beginning. In many ways, she knows what is best for me. And this battle is no longer one I can fight alone.

88

I finish my coffee and order another one. I cannot remember when I last sat alone in a café, and an unexpected feeling of quietude descends upon me. Afterwards I get up and continue my walk. Slow, unhurried, nothing like my usual pace. I eventually arrive at the Galleria Borghese—O. has wangled me a ticket at the last minute. I spend time in the company of Bernini, Caravaggio, and Canova. I am especially taken by Caravaggio's *David with the Head of Goliath* and Bernini's *Rape of Proserpina*. A luminous halo lights up David's face as he grabs Goliath's head—actually Caravaggio's last self-portrait: a beheaded man, dripping his final blood. In a small booklet I picked up at the entrance I read that, because Caravaggio had killed a man, he was sentenced to decapitation. He avoided it by fleeing to Naples, where the painting, re-enacting the murder, was executed. After that he lived continuously on the run. A penitent outlaw.

It is dark and disturbing, as is the Bernini sculpture: Pluto's' fingers dig into the stone flesh of his abducted victim as he attempts to overpower Proserpina and take her to the underworld. Her youthful face expresses fear and distress, and marbled tears run down her cheeks. I know about marbled tears. Eyes dry. Always dry.

But not here, in Rome.

The swell of those shadows is softly receding.

❀   ❀   ❀

There is a traffic jam on the Via Veneto. A taxi driver shouts at the car in front of him and honks his horn loudly. Soon several cars join in the honking chorus. A driver gets out of his Fiat and swears at no one in particular. I consult my map, turn off the main road, and leave the traffic and the swearing behind. Eventually I find myself on a small street off the Via Condotti—my sister has asked me to meet her nearby. I stop in front of an antique shop and gaze at a pair of exquisitely carved female masks: the women gaze back at me through eyes inlaid with lapis lazuli. There is something spectral about that ultramarine stare, which sends a shiver down my spine. It is as if those women, those eyes, were judging me. But judging what? My life so far? The road I have not taken?

I can see it, laid out before me like a field of laven-der, its spikes swaying in the wind.

I can see the dark purple of its flower. The blue green of its foliage. The fragrant field.

The wait.

There is activity in the adjacent designer shop, where two assistants have gathered around a woman who is clutching heavy bags. *La ringrazio Signora del Mosso, e buona giornata!* they cry out in an obse-quious manner—whatever it is their favourite client has purchased must have been substantial. Signora del Mosso, who is startingly beautiful, has luxuriant black hair; her tailored dress is unbuttoned just so, and she is wearing a strand of pearls around her neck. She brushes by me, seemingly unaware of my existence, as if I hadn't been standing in her line of vision, trying not to stare. Trying not to reveal that her world—of pedigree and privilege—is one I shall never inhabit, nor would I know how to if I tried.

Then I notice a man, presumably her husband. He has parked his expensive car and is running towards her. He is short and wiry. There is a large Rolex on his wrist. His face is red and angry. I hear him yell, Giulia! I see her lowering her bags to the pavement. She appears stunned. Fearful. And, before I know it, Rolex man is grabbing her by the arm and shouting so loudly that everyone on the street stops and stares as I do. I hear her cry out, *Pietro! per favore Pietro!* But Pietro is not in the mood for *favore*. His face is incandescent, and his hands now grasp her neck, as if he were going to strangle her. Giulia tries to push him away. She pleads in a throttled voice for him to let her go, her dignity and pedigree stripped away. She must be saved from the violence of this wild man. Why isn't anyone stepping in? Should I? Three people appear and suddenly they've surround-ed Pietro and torn him away from his wife, whose luxuriant hair has come undone. She is shaking uncontrollably, as I am, because this moment is a familiar one. I stroke my throat for Giulia and send words of courage flying in her direction, like a flock of carrier pigeons.

Pietro suddenly looks frightened, he is retreating now because more people have surrounded him, I hear someone mentioning that they are calling the police. *Vergogna!* A woman shouts. *Vergogna!*

Shame on you.

And shame has caught up with Pietro, who manages to break away from the crowd. He runs surprisingly fast towards his car and, before I know it, has driven away.

My eyes, like those of the shocked passers-by, are focused on Giulia. She pushes a few strands of her hair back into place, gathers her bags, and walks slowly away, head held high under the glare of that saffron sun.

89

The incident marked me. Pietro's violence and rage, the way it rendered obsolete all those thoughts of social inequality I had momentarily harboured: Signora del Mosso had been reduced to Giulia, a terrified woman who could not defend herself from her husband's violence.

I recount the incident to my sister, who surmises that Giulia was probably cheating on Pietro, and with reason. But how come no one called the police? This was clearly a case of domestic abuse. I thought the police had been called, I tell her. But it is possible that all those standing on the pavement were reluctant to accept that they were witnessing domestic abuse. Perhaps the fact that Giulia looked privileged somehow made it harder for the public to relate to her as a victim? My sister wonders too. Privilege can harm as well as protect, she says. It's a double-edged sword. Many things are double-edged in Italy, she sighs. They still have a lot of catching up to do.

We both wonder aloud what happened to Giulia after she went home. Did Pietro try throttling her again, or did he beg for forgiveness? And what if he wasn't her husband? Then who was he? He was her husband—he had to be. What I had witnessed was years of bottled-up resentment. He could no longer control himself. I could feel it. It was only going to get worse.

She was going to have to leave him.

I sent a lone carrier pigeon in her direction.

Leave him, Giulia.

Leave him.

90

That night my sister takes me to a restaurant overlooking the Piazza Farnese. Richard, an art critic and an old colleague of O.'s, is there with his wife Polly, an American divorcée with heavy eye makeup and musky perfume. There is also Anna, a colleague from the French Department, and Giorgia V., one of Italy's most famous novelists, whom I am told to sit next to. I have only read one of her books, which I didn't particularly like. But as I take my seat next to her, I wish I had given the other ones a chance. Before we arrived my sister told me that rumours about Giorgia had abounded for years. She was married to an electrician, a fact that didn't tally with her literary profile. She kept her husband well away from the public eye, or perhaps it was he who kept well away. Either way, she had seldom volunteered anything about him, apart from the fact that they had a son together. All this endeared her to me. But seeing her in the flesh has put paid to that initial sentiment. There is something intimidating about her. Her wild hair. Her beady eyes. The guttural sound of her laugh. She is disparaging to one of the waiters, who walks away looking upset. I wish I had understood what she said. She is now speaking to a young man who has stopped by our table, a fan presumably. He sounds nervous when he speaks and asks her something about her *ultimo libro*. Her last book. I wonder how many she's written. How the public will respond to my new novel. What if no one likes it? Is it too personal a story? Perhaps I should learn Italian. Leave London with my girls and start afresh. The word *fresh* conjures longings. The freedom of solitude. The newness of intimacy.

The smell of soil after rain.

A loud yap interrupts my thoughts. Giorgia owns a white terrier called Pootch, who is sitting under the table, and she is petting him repeatedly. *Pootchy pootchy caro mio*, she says. She explains to me that she takes Pootch everywhere and refuses to go to any restaurant that is not dog-friendly. Then she laughs and says that, actually, most restaurants these days allow Pootch to sit at her feet, just as he's doing now, because she, Giorgia, is very famous in Italy. And Pootch is such a nice dog! So polite, like a human being, she adds, patting him under the table one last time. Everyone loves him.

I don't, particularly. I care little about dogs and would much rather talk about books—which we eventually do. When I mention that I too am a writer, but not of her calibre of course, she appears interested. I explain that my second novel will be coming out soon. That the first one was a short-term success—which is not technically true, as it came out to some fanfare and was shortlisted for a couple of prizes. I was still receiving letters from admirers, and it was continuing to sell steadily. This was not the first time my modesty would backfire.

Giorgia presses me for details, and in a few words I describe the plot, the style, my inspirations. Her English is good despite a strong accent, and her enthusiasm for literature is infectious. But as the conversation meanders it becomes apparent that a barely concealed disdain for me has suddenly crept in. I am not sure why—is it because I used those words, *short-term success*? Do those words reveal a lowliness Giorgia cannot relate to? It is as if she has suddenly decided I am no longer worthy of conversation. Then it hits me: Giorgia is upset because, during the course of the discussion, I confessed to not having read her work. Yet! I had said, careful not to mention the book that I had read. But that adverb was not sufficient to dress the wounds of my error. There is no doubt that this is how she views it: as an unpardonable error. I turn my head towards her, prepared to say something redeeming—quite what, I'm not sure—but she is deep in conversation with my sister, her body leaning towards her, as far from me as possible, as if I smelled bad. Now I feel insulted. I had forgotten how needy certain writers could be. This one is not only needy but rude. I feel sorry for her husband.

Anna starts to speak to me. She is small and thin, with inquisitive, kohl-rimmed eyes. A strong French accent belies her fluent English. Anna is writing her thesis on Marguerite Duras and is delighted when I tell her that, like her, I am from Paris and that Duras is an author I've long admired. We slip into French and discuss Duras's merits. I find myself missing Paris. Missing my parents, my old friends, the language. Rueing the fact that my children speak only a few words. When Katia was small I spoke French to her. But my husband said he felt left out, so I gave up. It felt wrong, but I didn't want him to feel left out. When I later tried to make up for lost time it was too late: my girls were not interested. We like English better, they said.

Anna likes Duras's layering of voices and her elliptical sentences. The way she navigates the border between fact and fiction. Her way of writing about women. Anna quotes her: *Women must find their own answer. That's the important thing. I'm no longer interested in books about women written by men.* The two of us discuss further. How ahead of her time she was: Duras the anti-feminist-feminist. And men who write well about women? There are quite a few. Unlike Marguerite I won't give up reading them. I pick D. H. Lawrence, Chekhov, Henry James, and Tolstoy as examples. And Flaubert! Anna adds. Don't forget Flaubert.

I'm not forgetting him.

But what about your own answer? Have you found it? Anna asks me.

No, not yet. And you?

Same, she says. Or maybe I have but I just don't know it. Fuck merde.

We both laugh.

Fuck merde.

The conversation reminds me of my student days in Manhattan. I often think of the young woman I was then, of the notion of endless possibilities. It all seems long ago, though in actuality it is only a few years back. Perhaps I have become a different person, the possibilities less endless.

I was recently in touch with Claudia, whose brother died in 9/11. We spoke briefly, and everything about her sounded different, as if grief had turned her into another person. I was at a loss for words, and told her so. Before hanging up she said that she often thought of me. I would love to see you again, she said.

I wonder about taking a trip to New York. I could take the girls with me. Stay in a hotel, show them the sights. See Claudia, and my other friends from that time. And try to find Alexander. Is he there? A while back my mother mentioned that he was living between New York and Mexico. How she knew I wasn't sure. Someone in the art world had told my father, who had relayed the information. Anything to do with the Karlicks is always passed around, like a precious object. What happened that spring affected all of us apart from my sister, who was too young to take in the full gravity of the events: she does not give Alexander Karlick a second thought.

I tune into the conversations at the table. I can feel the wine inside me. I look at Richard and Anna, who are now laughing with Polly. Their heads are close together. Polly's food is still untouched. At one point she pushes a strand of her hair back. The diamond on her finger glitters.

Words unthread, floating like loose garments in an unspecified space.

I love artichokes.
Berlusconi is destroying this country.
My wife doesn't like the heat.
Valeria Messina è *una stronza*.
What does frizzante mean?
He was a revolutionary writer.
Add a bit of chili, but only at the end.
Near the Bastille.
Martha Stewart is a friend of mine. She's no embezzler.
But the question is: who owns Russia?
We went to the most wonderful hotel.
No, I live alone.
I love Andrew Caro. Karlick used to represent him, I think.
What? I interject. Did you just mention André Karlick?
Yes, why? Richard asks.
We used to know him and his family.

Two waiters arrive with the main dishes, which they place on the table. Vitello tonnato. Red snapper baked in salt. Bucatini all'amatriciana. Fried zucchini. Giorgia asks where Mauro is. I'm sure he'll be here soon. He's always late, my sister replies.

By then Richard has embarked on another conversation with Anna, and I see no point in pushing the Karlick angle, however much I want to. The moment has passed. No one knows how the sound of that name still elicits an instant response from me. Neither my sister nor this unlikely cast of characters she has surrounded herself with. Apart from Anna, money seems to play a paramount role in all their lives. It infiltrates their vocabulary as frequently as art and real estate. I do not know many people with money; I have spent most of my life working to make ends meet. But not my sister. Her husband comes from an affluent American family, and since she married him her circumstances have changed. Last summer the two of them were invited to stay with Richard and Polly, who own a large house in Palm Beach, which Giorgia declares to be a detestable little place. Everyone laughs apart from Polly, who seems insulted. Palm Beach is my home and it's anything but detestable, she says. When she takes a sip of her wine, her ring clinks angrily against the glass. I notice that Polly hasn't touched her food—she's always on a diet, I hear her husband complain. He refills my glass again. I'm drinking quickly. It's all because of Giorgia.

That's when Mauro arrives, dissolving the tension. He introduces himself to me, Richard, and Polly, and kisses everyone else on both cheeks. He grabs a chair and sits down next to me.

He has thick black hair, and probing eyes. Are they blue or brown? I cannot tell in the dark. He could be an artist, a poet. But I know he's a musician. I find him striking looking—for once my sister wasn't exaggerating. Sexy. A protruding Adam's apple, a wide smile. In no time the conversation is flowing between us, and it does not take me long to understand that the presence of this man has the potential to imperil my marriage. I have had several crushes in the past few years. Some heavier than others. Increasingly I fantasise about other men. I have always been faithful to my husband, but I know that I am vulnerable. That if I were to meet someone else, I would not be able to resist. And this man, sitting next to me at this Roman table, is the type of man I might not be able to resist.

My sister interrupts my thoughts and raises a glass in my honour: to Clara in Rome! All glasses are lifted now, and the wine is stirring inside me, as are those words: To Clara in Rome!

In front of the restaurant there are young men and women on scooters, their faces carefree, beautiful, their voices filling the night like an ancient song. Everything in this earthen city is like an ancient song. It reverberates inside me. I am not hard, as Paola has claimed. I am soft, often sad. Hardness is my armour. A knight's metal armour. Because my marriage is collapsing. I have tried to make it work, but it is collapsing. My shield against the world is porous. I have been starved of something I now understand to be happiness. And here, in Rome, I can feel it rise within the city walls. In the sing-song sound of the city's words. In the food I just ate—the pungent flesh of the tomatoes, the spicy olives, the fragrant basil leaves. In the smell of jasmine which lingers in the air.

Rising like water through cracked earth.

91

Come for a drink with me, Mauro says, after the dinner is over.

Everyone has left. We are the last customers. We have continued speaking to each other long after the plates have been cleared. The waiters are tired. I can tell they would like us to go home.

But I've had plenty to drink, I tell him. I cannot have more.

Come with me and don't drink, he says.

He wears a wedding band.

We both do.

92

We walk for about five minutes, then he stops in front of a nondescript building. A cocktail den, he calls it, opening the door and motioning me to follow him down a flight of stairs.

It is dimly lit, with sleek chairs and giant chandeliers. Techno music is playing in the background. A waiter comes to take our order. My knees are knocking. I wonder what has got into me. Everything, I decide, as Mauro orders two caipirinhas. Everything has got into me.

He asks about my life. My sister has told him a few things. That I'm a writer, that I have two children and live in London. Yes, that's right, I answer. There is not much more to say.

I suddenly wonder what I'm doing there. Mauro can feel it as well, I can tell. I'm married too, he says. I'm not in the habit of inviting women for late night drinks in cocktail dens. I just thought it would give us a chance to talk some more. I liked talking to you before, he adds.

I nod. So did I.

In the restaurant, Mauro told me how he used to earn a living as a tour guide before concentrating full time on the cello. He had grown up an only child in Rome, in a working-class family. Classical music was not their world. But he had dreamt of playing the cello ever since he had seen a boy play it on television, when he was nine years old. His father disapproved, but his mother saved money in secret for him to start lessons. Those lessons paid off, and he eventually won a scholarship to the Mannes School of Music in the US. He had never left Italy before that. He met his wife there, a violinist. They formed a string quartet together, with two friends. They moved to Rome, where he gave cello lessons and briefly became a tour guide to get by. But his wife was not happy in Rome. Eventually she stopped performing with the quartet and moved back to the US, where she is now. Things are a bit problematic between us, Mauro admits. I'm not sure what's going to happen there. It's not easy to maintain a transatlantic relationship.

He also mentions that his quartet will be performing in Reading the following week. Maybe we could meet up in London?

Maybe.

The waiter arrives with the drinks, and after a while I no longer wonder what I'm doing there. Nothing will happen between us because we're both married.

Even if things are a bit problematic with his wife. I don't wish to find out why that's the case. And for all I know he could be lying. He wouldn't be the first one to use so-called marital problems as seduction bait. I shall not fall for it. But I am drunk, and my mouth feels dry. And his wife has stayed behind, in the US. Therefore, he is probably telling the truth.

Mauro's dark eyes rest on mine. The attraction between us is undeniable. In my eleven years of marriage, nothing like this has happened to me. Nothing. Mauro wears a white shirt which seems to glow in the dark, as if it were fluorescent. Or perhaps he's the fluorescent one. Mauro Cassano, the fluorescent one. That's his name. I wonder if his lips glow.

There's something ethereal about you, he begins.

I stop him. I must go home.

Of course, he says.

He walks me to a cab. Before I get in, he grabs my hand and kisses it.

The taxi drives away into the darkness.

His lips.

That night I dream of the masked women from the antique shop. Their lapis lazuli stare wakes me with a start. I might even have screamed. And it isn't only their eyes. Their mouths, too. The women are saying something to each other in a language I cannot comprehend. They could be talking about me; it's hard to tell. But their eyes are boring into mine, unflinching.

93

On the way back, at Rome's Fiumicino Airport, I buy a few things for the children. Lindt chocolates, a carved wooden box for Katia, a bracelet for Lola. I am queuing for the till when I notice an older man in front of me, holding a bottle of whisky and a carton of cigarettes. He has white hair and is a little hunched. An overly made-up woman stands by his side.

At one point the man turns round and briefly looks at me.

I know those eyes. I know that icy blue.

It has got to be him: an older, but still dapper, André Karlick.

André? I ask, before I can stop myself.

He looks at me quizzically. Yes? Do I know you?

I tell him who I am. I mention my parents. I don't mention his son.

André breaks into a large smile. But of course! he exclaims, shaking my hand warmly. How are you? How are your parents? You're beautiful, he adds. Congratulations.

The woman by his side extends her hand. Zusi, she says. André's wife.

At least it sounds like Zusi. She is short and wears several chunky gold necklaces.

We both pay for our purchases and walk out into the terminal together. André asks more questions, about me, my children, my parents, and tells me about himself. I live in Switzerland now, he says. I lead a wonderfully peaceful existence.

How nice, I say, as the words hit me like bullets.

Then he mentions Alexander. Do you remember Alexander? We all had lunch together, at the Café des Artistes.

Yes, I remember him, I answer coolly.

He lives in Mexico City. Has been there for a few years now, doing very well. Married, two children, lovely boys, lovely wife.

I don't tell him that I know. Not about the children, but Mexico.

He's an art dealer like me, André continues. He's opened his own gallery.

André pauses and looks at me. If you ever go to Mexico, you must get in touch with Alexander. He's in New York often too, about once a month. He'd be delighted to see you again. He doesn't tend to come to London much, André adds, his voice dropping ever so slightly.

No, of course.

Why don't you give me your details? I'll pass them on.

He pulls a card out of his wallet. His name is embossed on a creamy background.

His wife hands me a pen which she digs out of her bag. Her necklaces jangle as she does so. I scribble my name and number and hand the card back to André, together with the pen. Something tells me Alexander will never see it: his father will forget or lose the card.

We part ways. André kisses me goodbye affectionately, as does his wife.

I'm so pleased you recognised me, he says. Very good to run into you. Please send my love to your family.

I will.

And I'll be sure to tell Alexander I saw you! he shouts, as he walks towards the departure gate.

I wave back and turn quickly away.

I find an empty seat away from the crowds.

All thoughts of Mauro Cassano have been entirely banished from my mind. All thoughts about my husband too.

I clasp the presents for the children against my chest, head lowered towards my knees. I cry quietly, hoping no one will notice. At one point I sense a presence nearby. I look up briefly to see a small boy holding a teddy bear, staring at me. His mother appears and pulls him away.

Come over here, Alexander, she says. Leave the lady alone.

94

I no longer love my husband. I have fallen—dropped, tumbled, plummeted—out of love. I would have thought that the pace of the process would be similar to that of falling in love. Slow, tentative, a dawning revelation. But this is no dawning revelation. I am having coffee one morning. I see him sitting at his computer with his suit on. His glasses are slipping down his nose. He suffers from alopecia, and the round patch in the centre of his scalp is a faintly nauseating peach-colour. He is about to go to a meeting. He is nervous. His lips move imperceptibly. I look at him and feel nothing. I realise that I have felt nothing for a long time. The revelation shocks me. That, despite feeling nothing, I stayed married to him. Shared his bed. And that, while I was doing so, the change must have been happening gradually. Stealthily. And now it is over. My emotional pockets are empty. I have stopped loving him. Stopped loving the man he has become. Therefore I must leave him. I am unhappy. If I do not leave now, I will never be free. I will be stuck with him until there is no strength in me at all. And, for the sake of my children, I cannot let that happen.

Because if I stay, my story will become theirs.

A dysfunctional future.

95

Doors.
Timber. Glass. Steel.
Women and doors.
Creaking.
Opening.
Slamming.
Women tiptoeing walking hurrying
running bolting fleeing.

My own wooden panel.
I am not sure I can do it.
Leaving requires planning.
I haven't planned.
But I must leave.

Mauro rings me on my mobile while I'm eating lunch with my husband and Lola. I don't answer, and emit a forced sigh of irritation.

Who's that?

A friend of my sister's. He wants me to go to his concert. He and his wife play in a string quartet. But it's in Reading. I'm not going to go to Reading.

My husband scrutinizes my face. OK, he says. How do you know this guy?

I told you. He's a friend of my sister's. I met him last week in Rome.

What's his name?

Mauro Cassano. He's a cellist. But I'm not interested in going to Reading. Or in hearing him play.

That seems a bit harsh.

It's not harsh. I'm just busy, that's all.

I look at my husband. What's the matter?

Nothing.

Lola fiddles with her alphabet pasta. I found a P and an A! she squeals, lifting the letters from her plate.

Papa. *Papapapapapa*.

97

I read about Giorgio Morandi. How he lived all of his life in Bologna, in an apartment with his mother and three sisters. His bedroom doubled as his studio. He hardly ever left the city, and never visited a foreign country. He was known as *Il Monaco*. The Monk. He was a private, quiet man who never married or had children. He was probably a virgin. When he wanted to find out about the outside world, he relied on books and the black and white postcards he collected. He once said that he was fortunate enough to lead an uneventful life. The fact that he saw this as fortunate strikes me. Yet that is how he lived. He painted all his works—still lifes, self-portraits, flowers, vases—in his studio. After he died in 1964, the studio was pre-served as he had left it. His stained apron hanging on a hook. The objects he painted: bottles, vases, jugs. His paintbrushes. An easel in a corner. His old hat. *One can travel this world and see nothing*, he wrote.

With his paintbrush, Morandi was able to create a world outside his line of vision. And despite the limitation and 'uneventful' nature of his subject mat-ter, those small still lifes became universal. Their colours vibrate, as does their stillness.

I cannot help but wonder how differently Morandi might have painted had he seen the lavender fields of Provence. The skyscrapers of New York. The streets of Paris. The ochre red of the Atlas Mountains. The cobalt blue of the Aegean Sea. I suspect there would have been a tremolo within that stillness. That his line of vision would have been forever altered.

I would like to alter my line of vision. To seek a tremolo.

98

We meet up the day after his concert. I would in fact have loved to hear Mauro perform. But it was logis-tically impossible, as my husband was suspicious— and home. Now he's gone to Germany for a meeting, and Mauro is waiting for me in a Notting Hill café. I haven't seen him in broad daylight before. His eyes are the colour of chestnuts. His skin is light brown. He is even better looking than I remembered.

I don't think I can do this, I say quickly. When you called yesterday my husband was right there. We were eating lunch with my daughter. I told him you were performing with your wife. But you're not.

I have come to my senses. No matter what's happen-ing at home, I cannot give in to my desires. It will only make things worse.

I'm not sure what you're talking about. We're not

doing anything, Mauro assures me. We're having a friendly cup of coffee. We're adults. We're both married. And no, I wasn't performing with my wife.

I sit with him for about thirty minutes. I am very nervous. He offers me a cigarette and I take it. I don't remember him smoking last time.

We discuss his concert, which went well. He's in London for forty-eight hours. A friend, the patron of the string quartet, is organising a dinner for the musicians. Would you like to come? he asks. It's tonight, at 7.30, in his beautiful Mayfair townhouse.

Just as I'm about to answer my phone rings: my husband. My heart beats more quickly than it should. I don't answer but wonder why he's calling me—he seldom does these days.

I must go, I tell Mauro. I'm really sorry. And no, I can't come to the dinner tonight. But thank you for asking me. I'm sure it will be great.

He takes a puff of his cigarette and looks at me. This is not as complicated as you think it is, he says. But if seeing me makes you feel uncomfortable, I understand.

Yes, it makes me feel uncomfortable.

I must leave now because if I do not, I will give in. I will follow him to his hotel. I will ride the lift in silence to the fifth floor. A person will join us on the first floor and leave on the third. Mauro will move slowly towards me. He will touch my cheek with his warm hand. We will arrive on the fifth floor. I will tell him that I must leave. I cannot do this. Mauro will take hold of my hand, just as I'm about to dash back to the lift.

Come here.

He will murmur my name and push the door to the room open. I will barely notice what it looks like, except that the bed is very large. He will close the door and kiss me against its frame. His tongue will be hot. He will undress me in a frenzy, and we will fall onto the bed. I will feel myself being lifted to a place I haven't visited in a long time. A place of longing so intense I might cry. A place where skin melds with skin, hunger with hunger. Ravenous.

Sublime.

99

We will not see each other again. If we do, I will want him. And I cannot want him. We will part ways in front of the Notting Hill Tube. I will not kiss him or say goodbye. We are two strangers, heading home to our everyday lives.

I decide that the only way for me to move forward is to pretend that this never happened. And it didn't. Nothing has happened. I made it all up.

We sat in a café and I went home, because I was feeling uncomfortable.

But now I wish that I had stayed.

100

I am wearing a black skirt and an ivory shirt with flared sleeves. I have accepted his invitation and am standing in the middle of a crowded and expensive Mayfair room. A far cry from Mauro's Roman childhood. His mother would have been proud to see her son surrounded by such wealth. Such success. Waiters are serving champagne and canapes. The walls are covered in Old Master paintings. One of them depicts a view of a lone boat on a river. My eye is drawn to the shadows, the curves, the reflection of light on water. And then someone taps me on the shoulder. I turn round and there is Mauro, in a suit and tie. How are you? He smiles. I'm so glad you decided to come.

My cheeks burn. My lips burn. Everything about me burns.

A man announces that dinner is served. Please take your seats.

We continue to make small talk. We are not ready to take our seats. I am listening to Mauro, who is telling me about his day in London. Then he mentions that his wife is very sorry she couldn't be there. Sometimes she misses playing with us, he tells me.

I find that strange. Why would he impart that unnecessary information? Then, in a slightly worried tone, he asks about my husband.

He's away, I tell him. Until tomorrow.

A woman comes and interrupts our conversation. Or is it a conversation? It seems to be more a pair of parallel monologues. His and mine.

A two-way monologue of supressed desire.

I have been seated next to him.

For one moment, one very brief moment, I contemplate asking to be moved elsewhere. But it is too late. He smiles as he pulls his seat out and sits down, after me. He introduces himself to the man on my left, a film director. They speak Spanish to each other. I didn't know Mauro spoke Spanish; he sounds fluent. Actually I hardly know anything about him, so why should I be surprised?

I drink too quickly and leave my food untouched. I listen to Mauro speak. He is telling me about his last tour in Germany. Sold out every night, he says. The Germans like us. We perform there a lot.

I don't know much about classical music, although I enjoy listening to it. It's the only music my father likes, I tell him. I should meet him then, Mauro quips. I'm not sure that's a good idea, I laugh. In fact, nothing about the evening is a good idea. But it is too late to backtrack. The conversation veers towards other matters. The little boat he owns, which is moored in Sicily, next to his cousin's house. I like the idea that he owns a little boat. Somehow the boat segues into my childhood. I tell him about Paris, my time in New York, my college years. He listens quietly. His eyes take things in so deeply it is as if my words were reflected in his irises. I wonder about his wife, but don't dare ask him. The Spanish producer attempts conversation with me. We exchange a few words, then I return to Mauro. I don't mind if the producer looks vaguely insulted that he has been left on his own. The seat beside him has remained vacant all along. Eventually he gets up and leaves the table. Mauro asks about my husband, but I don't tell him the truth. That our marriage has reached a dead end. In fact, there is nothing left between us. Only a vast gap where the air blows cold. There is me, there is him, but the *us* has been sawn off, like rotten wood.

It's a complicated situation, I say instead.

I'm sorry. It's a bit the same with Gaby and me. A complicated situation.

Gaby and me.

A waiter pours me another glass of wine. Soon I will be drunk. Unless I already am. What is it about this man? I've met him twice and overdid it on the alcohol both times. It is unlike me. Something about him destabilises me. I must watch what I tell him. I am saying things I shouldn't. And now the patron is making a speech. Sebastian something or other. He reads from a sheet of paper and his signet ring shines under the light above him. The speech is boring and my mind wanders. I've asked Silvia, the babysitter, to put the children to bed early. I hope she has. Lola is going to the Transport Museum the following day. I want her to get a good night's sleep. And Katia has a Maths test. She's asked for help, but I couldn't provide it. I've never been good at Maths. I'm hoping Silvia will be able to step in, as she did last time. Matematica is my thing, she said. She comes from L'Aquila, in the Abruzzo. I live on a fault line, she once told me. I know about earthquakes. The seismic risk is high where we are. But we're not leaving.

Silvia is studying to be an anthropologist. She wears large glasses that make her eyes look small. She's slightly overweight and is prone to wearing unflattering clothing. *Sono grossa*, she says, patting her belly. When I'm no longer *grossa* I will wear nice clothes like you do.

We all love Silvia. Her cooking, her humour, her warmth.

Silvia who lives on a fault line.

Sebastian is now making a toast, which is followed by loud applause. Then the violinist makes a speech. She has a Russian accent and a humour about her which Sebastian did not have. I wonder what Mauro thinks of him. I wonder what Mauro thinks of me. Then I feel his hand sliding up my leg. He slowly lifts the hem of my skirt and caresses my knee.

I begin to tremble as his hand works its way up my thigh.

I reach out to stop him and he grabs my hand.

You're so beautiful, he says. I'm sorry. I can't stop myself. I'm sorry.

Our fingers remain intertwined.

101

He is staying in a friend's apartment off Kensington High Street. Not a hotel room then. We wait for a taxi together. It is raining. I don't speak. The alcohol is impairing my decision-making. What am I doing, exactly?

We walk towards a bus stop in order to shelter from the increasingly heavy rain. It is just the two of us.

I must go home, I tell him.

Of course, he replies.

He pulls me towards him and kisses me. He swirls his tongue in my mouth and I feel his hands searching for more of me. I stop him.

Slowly, I say.

Slowly.

The taxi drops us off near Hyde Park. I follow him in silence in the night and the rain. I keep my head lowered. The apartment is in a tall mansion block. Although it is unlikely, I dread bumping into someone I know. We take the lift to the top floor. My feet are wet, as is my hair. Part of me wants to disappear with him, part of me wants to flee.

I don't know, I whisper as he fumbles for his keys.

I do, he answers. And I think you do too.

102

There is a magnificent view of London from the apartment. The buildings glow like lanterns. The sound of a police siren rips momentarily through the air. I can make out the London Eye, the Shard. The lighting is dim, and the room we are standing in is plainly furnished, like a hotel. I turn towards him. I begin to say something, but he kisses me just as I'm about to speak. My words get lost between his lips. When he stops, I find myself asking him to kiss me again. It isn't me speaking, but another voice. It isn't me kissing him, but another woman, another me.

We're inside the bedroom now. David Gray is singing in the background.

There's no rhyme or reason to love. This sweet, sweet love.

Our clothes are on the floor, in a heap. He clasps me against him. He kisses me, over and over. His hands glide over me. Then his lips. Against my neck, circling my nipples, my thighs. He whispers words of lust and longing. *My oh my*, sings David Gray. Now he is parting my legs and sliding into me.

I can't get enough of you, he whispers.

I can't get enough of you, he whispers again.

It is dawn by the time I get home. My clothes are crumpled, my underwear is wet. I still feel a bit drunk.

I can hear Silvia in the next room. She has slept over. I called her from the Mayfair townhouse. I'm far from London, I lied. I will be home very late.

I close my eyes.

The intensity of my pleasure. The tenderness and ardency of his lovemaking.

I had forgotten what tenderness and ardency felt like.

White-hot tenderness.

103

I wake up with a start. How long did I sleep? A few hours at most. I jump out of bed and grab last night's blue lace underwear. I look for a box of matches and find one in the sitting room. I take the underwear back to the bedroom and strike a match: I must burn it. Then I think better of it. I run into the kitchen and search for a pair of scissors. I cut the underwear into little pieces. I cut the night into little pieces. I shove the pieces into a plastic bag and place the bag in the bin.

But what if my husband decides to look in the bin? I cannot put anything past him.

I throw on a pair of trousers, a jumper, slippers. I rush outside. I walk a few blocks until I find a bin, and I throw the plastic bag inside.

A woman with cheap highlights is smoking a cigarette, leaning against her car. I find myself asking her for one. She lights it for me, and I thank her. It is barely 7.00 a.m., I am smoking a cigarette, and I fear my husband far more than I ever have before. I fear that last night's deed is written on my face. I fear what he might do if he reads it. I take a last drag in front of the building and stamp the cigarette out on the ground. I go back inside the apartment. It is quiet and I enter on tiptoe.

Katia barges into my bedroom just as I'm about to

get into the shower. She is wearing stripy pink pyjamas, and her curly blonde hair looks knotty.

What are you doing? she asks. How come you're already dressed?

I came home late, I answer. I didn't sleep very well. I'm going to take a shower now. And you shouldn't come in here without knocking.

Katia mumbles something indistinct and leaves the room. I tear my clothes off and jump into the shower. I scrub my skin until it turns red. But nothing can wash the night away. It is indelible. I have done this because I sought tenderness. Not vengeance. Tenderness.

White-hot tenderness.

104

My husband and I are arguing about something anodyne. And suddenly it comes out. That I would like to separate. I can no longer hold it in. That neither of us is happy with the other. That there is no point in staying together anymore. That I am certain he feels the same. That our marriage has reached a dead end.

He says nothing for a while. He is sitting on the sofa, his knees tightly pressed together. He asks if there is anyone else. His voice sounds different. As if he has already stopped knowing me.

No. There is no one else.

He asks it again. Are you telling me the truth?

Yes, I am, I reply.

He leaves the room and slams the door behind him. Moments later I hear a crash. I rush to find him standing in the kitchen, smashed plates by his feet, broken bits of porcelain covering the floor. My favourite wedding plates, a gift from my parents, which I have cherished all these years.

I shake and shout. Why would you do such a thing? Why? Why?

Please get out, he says, in a quivering voice. Get out and leave me the fuck alone.

I don't leave him alone. I remain there and we scream at each other. Scream and cry as I hold a broken plate between my hands. Words fly across the room like invisible objects. I can feel their weight crushing me. We have both become exposed strangers, beset by a molecular rage. Amid the rage is long buried pain. Words of truth but also contrition. At one point my husband asks if I still love him.

No. I'm sorry.

It comes out of my mouth easily. I feel neither sadness nor regret. Only relief.

Leave me alone, he repeats, in a composed voice this time.

As I walk away I see him open the kitchen closet. He picks up a broom and starts to sweep the shattered remnants of the plates into a pile.

105

We have agreed to part amicably. We must, for the children's sake.

Part. Amicably.

Gentle words that detonate. Oxymoronic words. Jagged porcelain words.

We have told the children. That their parents are going to live apart for a while.

For how long? they ask.

We don't know.

106

The movers have arrived. It has been two weeks since I made the decision. Katia has stopped eating. They are taking away our belongings in cardboard boxes and Katia has stopped eating.

Lola kisses her father goodbye. She cries.

But you'll be back my darling, my husband says, comforting her.

Katia doesn't speak. She stands stiffly, with down-cast eyes.

You'll be back, my husband repeats, heartbroken.

The sun is shining. I walk towards the door, carrying our suitcases. I open it.

I let my daughters walk in front of me. I stop and look at the door one last time.

I close it slowly behind me.

107

My new apartment is in Camden. A top floor, two-bedroom apartment with a view of the London rooftops. The elitist, leftist North London my husband has always hated. Except that there is nothing elitist about the apartment I have found, or the street on which it is located. A couple of unsavoury types live next door, but they are harmless, I am assured. Smoke lots of weed and keep to themselves, that sort of thing.

I don't mind them, or the music that they sometimes play at full blast. On one occasion I cannot resist singing along to a song. My upstairs neighbour is shouting "shut up!" and there I am, standing by my window dancing to Al Green's "Take Me to the River". It is midnight and I am happy and dancing, and my children are small. Ten and five years old. Small and sad. Sad and angry. We don't like it here, they say. We don't like the view. We don't like the rooftops. We want to go home.

When evening falls, the rooftops are bathed in a pink hue. The bells from a church chime in the distance. They are a great comfort to me, but not to Katia. Their chime marks the beginning or the end of a moment in time. And that moment reverberates deep inside my daughter. It is the sound of a separation, but also of something new and tentative, which feels confusing to her, because newness divides her loyalty. It breaks her heart, which in turn breaks mine. I have caused her suffering. But there was no alternative. I feel free now. I have been given a chance to recover what has been lost.

108

Katia has slowly started eating again. But her stomach hurts. Every day, she says. I send her to school anyway. One morning I receive a phone call that my daughter is unwell. I must come and pick her up. She has complained of acute abdominal pains. She must be taken to hospital. I rush to school and take her straight to the emergency room. Her face is as white as chalk. But by the time I arrive the pain has abated. She has regained colour in her cheeks. The doctor examines her nonetheless. There is no indication of anything serious, he declares. Your daughter is fit and healthy.

On the way back, Katia tells me that the doctor was wrong. It is serious and it is all because of me. It's your fault, she says. Everything is your fault because you left my Daddy.

109

I devote myself entirely to my girls. I tell them they must see their father as much as they want to. The power of that modal verb takes me—and them—by surprise: *must*. If they must, they shall. And as they do, their pain slowly eases to a more manageable place. Their loyalties might be divided, but not the love their parents have for them. There is a fine balance to be struck. I can hear it in the sound of Katia's voice, which has become steadier. Lighter. And Lola is singing again.

110

I agree to meet up with their father for a Sunday lunch. We haven't had a meal together in a long time, and the girls fuss over what to wear.

Katia favours trousers, while for Lola it is dresses only. But they have both asked for their shoes to be polished for the occasion—I'm a good shoe polisher, my girls tell me. Before we left the flat, they watched me clean their leather moccasins with a damp rag and buff them with a brush to make them shine. When the procedure was over, the girls applauded and fought over whose moccasins were the shinier.

Now we are walking down Kensington High Street together, like a normal family on its way to a Sunday lunch. My girls' shoes are shining, the sun is emerging from behind the clouds. My husband has grabbed my hand, which surprises me—we're way past holding hands. I try to pull it away, but he then crushes my fingers together so hard that they crack, like nuts. A spike-like pain shoots through me. I am in shock and cry out for him to stop, but his gaze is focused ahead, his hand still gripping mine while my daughters walk ahead, utterly unaware of what is happening. I shout again. What are you doing? Are you crazy?

He immediately removes his hand, and Katia turns round. Are you all right, Mummy? She sounds worried. What's happening? Why did you just shout?

My husband smiles broadly. She's fine, Katia, don't worry. Everything is fine.

I look at him and his fake, broad smile.

Everything is not fine, I say, trying to steady my voice. I think you should have lunch without me.

I'm clutching my hand now, and it is all I can do not to cry.

I cannot tell my daughters the truth. But then I find a way.

Your father is not happy today, I say. And he doesn't want Mummy to be happy either.

The girls exclaim—no! no! that's not true!—and my husband looks mortified. Until now I have been careful to shield my daughters from his darker side. He replies that of course it's not true and asks them to be sweet and wait by the restaurant at the end of the street, right there, he points, no crossing required. One minute my darlings, he says, just one minute. I need to talk to your mother.

Katia runs off with Lola. They stop by the canopy of the restaurant, and I can see them huddled together, whispering to each other, pointing at us. The pain in my hand is such that I fear my husband might have broken it. Why do I still refer to him as *my husband*? My X-husband. Who is now telling me that I must have lunch with them. That it is vital the two of us maintain cordial appearances for the sake of the children. Not doing so could damage them greatly.

Cordial appearances? Did you really mean that?

He is standing by my side, a flash of alarm in his eyes as I spew invectives at him. Words I have no control over spill out of my mouth and I do nothing to stop them. I say things I have never said before, with the language he knows best: brutal, contemptuous, cutting. I no longer fear him. I have lost all respect for him. If anything, I harbour a deep pity for him, Pity for the life he has attempted and failed to build for himself. Pity too for my puny voice during all those years when it could have been so much louder. If only I had known that it was not the door that mattered, but the handle. A quick, deft turn to the outside.

I mention the lawyer whom I visited the previous day. How she was going to draw up a custody agreement. How, although I had hesitated before seeing her, I can now see how imperative it is that I protect our children. They should never again be subjected to their father's bouts of insanity—neither should I. Precautions must be taken. They can visit him, but on my terms.

My husband looks astounded. You can't do that, he says, his voice faltering. You can't. And I'm really sorry I hurt your hand, he adds. I don't know what got into me. I'm just very upset. Your leaving me has been so fucking difficult. And it only happened a month ago. So please don't involve a lawyer yet. Please. It's way too soon.

No, it's not.

He is speaking quickly now, imploring me to give him another chance. The girls are all I have left! he cries out. But I'm not interested in his cries. All I want to do is go home. Be as far away from him and his words as possible.

And now my daughters are running towards us. Katia, followed by Lola.

We didn't want to wait anymore, Katia says, speaking breathlessly. And we don't like being left on our own. It's actually against the law, do you know that? For parents to leave their children like you did. Talking like that, so far away from us.

Her eyes are shooting darts at me. But not her father.

We didn't break the law and we didn't leave you on your own, I state firmly. We could see you perfectly well. You were twenty or so metres away from us.

Mummy! Lola exclaims. She runs towards me and into my arms. Her cheeks are red and her eyes are shining. Me and Katia we're hungry! she cries out, her small arms encircling my waist.

I explain that I won't be joining them for lunch after all. Something important has come up and I must go home. But they'll have a lovely lunch with their father. He'll take very good care of them.

What? But what has come up? Lola is no longer hugging me. She appears startled. Distressed. As is her sister. They raise their voices, and a few passers-by turn round and stare.

I'll explain when we get home, I reassure them. Nothing to worry about. But I need to rush back. Daddy will take very good care of you, I repeat. You can order all the pizza you like. And that chocolate cake.

But we want you to be with us, Lola says, and her eyes fill with tears. We want you to eat the pizza and the chocolate cake with us, Mummy. Like a family.

I nearly give in. The pain is overwhelming. The guilt. My girls are being punished along with their father for his sins. But punished he must be. Otherwise this will happen again. I know him well enough. He has always been a man who forgets easily.

I am suddenly overcome by the urge to speak French. And I do. I tell the girls a few things I know they will not understand. About my devotion to them, but also about their father. They look at me quizzically—why are you speaking French like that, Mummy?—as if their mother has gone mad. But I haven't. I am sane, and I need French to feel it.

I hug and kiss them goodbye and switch back to English. I tell my girls that I love them. Please do this for me, I say, lowering my voice so that only they can hear me. Have a delicious lunch and then you can tell me all about it when you get home, and we'll watch a movie together. Even two!

Which ones? Katia asks, despite herself.

Any ones you like.

OK, they say, nodding their heads in unison. OK.

But their voices sound small.

I walk away quickly. A torrent of tears streams down my cheeks. Then it stops, because I have heard something. My name is being called. It is Katia. She must not see me cry. I have to get a grip on myself. I wipe my eyes, breathe in deeply, and turn around.

But there is no one there.

111

Mauro has been in touch, but I don't reply to his messages. On the phone I told my sister that I had met up with him for coffee. That he had mentioned problems with his wife. My sister sounded flummoxed. I think you must have misunderstood, she declared. Gaby did not return to the US because she was unhappy in Rome, but because she had been asked to join the Chicago Philharmonic. Didn't Mauro tell you? That's so weird. And she couldn't turn down the Philharmonic. Of course she couldn't. Who could resist such an offer? I'm sure you misunderstood what he said, she repeated. Gaby is his whole life.

❀   ❀   ❀

A few months later I bumped into Mauro at a friend's party in London. He was there with Gaby. I tried to make a quick exit, but he stopped me. Hello! he exclaimed, a little too heartily. He introduced me to his wife as a friend from the old days. Gaby shook my hand warmly. She was very tall, with sharp cheekbones and short hair. Her voice was husky, as was her laugh. She was a good woman, I could tell. She had no idea that her husband was a liar. That we were not friends from the old days. That his eyes were a wandering brown. Chances were he was no stranger to conjugal lapses. I didn't need my sister to confirm it. I had realised that in retrospect, thinking of our night together: his manner was overly confident. As if he had done it before, inside that same flat, with other women.

But he did it well. Very well.

His lips against mine. Him, inside me. How he had pressed me against the wall as he took me from behind. How he had whispered, *I can't get enough of you.*

The sheets in a heap at dawn.

A man she knew approached Gaby and she excused herself. Mauro took the opportunity to try and speak to me alone, but I cut him off. I have to go. Please don't try to contact me.

Wait! He tried to hold me back, but I fled. An email

arrived in my inbox that evening, but I ignored it. I didn't hear from him again until my book launch, a few months later. A message appeared on my phone and I read it before realising it was from Mauro. It said how sorry he was to be missing my launch. He would have loved to be there. He was so glad he had received an invitation. He was looking forward to reading my book. He hoped we could be friends and put the past behind us.

An invitation? The last person I wanted to see was Mauro. He had lied in order to lure me into his bed. Then again, perhaps I had let myself be lured. Did it really matter whether he was having problems with his wife? All I had wanted was to forget, for one night only, about the marital life I would soon leave behind. In Mauro's arms I had found what I was seeking. The validation of my eroded femininity.

And it had left me yearning for more.

112

In an unopened box in my Camden flat, I discover a stash of photographs.

Here is my father holding me on his knee, smiling. I must be four or five years old. My hair is curly and blonde, like Katia's. I wear a blue pinafore dress and black patent leather shoes. In the background is my mother, gazing at the scene wistfully. I detect a sadness in her eyes, as if she was feeling left out. I wonder if she did, and, if so, how often. Life was not easy with my father. But no matter the difficulties, she always protected him. He's working hard, she would say. You must show your father respect. The fact that her job was equally hard, and that she was owed the same amount of respect, was deemed inconsequential. But she never complained. She was mother first, translator second. And, unlike our father's, when she worked her door was always open.

A picture slips out of a yellowed envelope. Three

young women in the 1980s. Nadine, Hélène, and me sitting outside La Palette, the café that we frequented for most of our adolescence. I must be fifteen or sixteen years old. We are all smoking cigarettes, looking happy. I don't remember who took the photograph. Perhaps it was Sophie, whom I have never heard from again. Nadine looks the same as she does today, years later. Elegant and serious. Hélène is wearing a mini dress and large hooped earrings. She appears older than any of us—perhaps she always did. Hélène predictably married at twenty-two, had four children, and moved to the Far East with her husband. Then she divorced and moved back to Paris, her children in tow. She was now training to become a yoga teacher. This is what Nadine told me. Her path did not turn out as she thought it would, she added.

I replied that it often didn't. Life is divided into two paths: the one before us and the one behind us. This was who I was at the time of that photograph. I was contemplating the path before me. Sitting in that café, in deep conversation with my friends. Pretending to be confident and composed when in fact I was neither. My ideas were still condensing. I dreamt of self-assertion and self-discovery. Of truth. Truth meant balance. I was certain of it. I felt unbalanced, fragmented like those distorted women in Picasso's portraits. Olga. Dora. Marie-Thérèse. Fernande. But then I left the parental fold and entered the vortex of the unknown. One day I would write about that. Freedom and pain. The collision between my life story and the one I had imagined for myself. The slow reassembly of those fragments into a whole.

Here I am with my husband, holding hands and laughing. We're in France for our honeymoon, near the Spanish border. I wear a white dress and espadrilles. My hair is flying in my face. Time feeds memory and memory feeds time. A muted, vague outline of a woman I once knew appears. I hold the photograph of that woman between my fingers, freeze-framing a life that is no longer mine. I stare and she stares back. Who are you? I ask her. She is me and she is not. I want little to do with her, but I cannot deny her existence. She is the mother of my children. She lives within my flesh, a new woman with an old story. In this one, the wind was blowing, and she was laughing, unaware that she was standing on the edge of a precipice. Or perhaps she was aware of it but refused to admit it. So she pretended that everything was fine.

Until she could no longer.

113

My mother rings to say that she has just received a phone call from André Karlick, of all people. She hadn't heard from him in years. Perhaps twenty years. He sounded just the same. Kind voice. According to André, Alexander was coming to London and wanted to see me and asked for my number. So she gave it to André. She hopes that was OK. One never knows with you, she adds.

Of course it's OK, I answer, feeling something dislodge inside me.

He was a lovely boy. Do you remember that day when we all had lunch together? And then he came by to get something from the apartment?

Yes of course I do.

I swallow hard and sit down. Did he say when he was coming to London?

I don't think so, no, she answers after a short pause. Just that it would be soon.

Something important will happen if I see Alexander again. I am not sure what, only that it will be important. Or perhaps I'm projecting. It is one of my foibles, projecting. And I've done plenty of that with Alexander.

I flick through my memories of him. A flimsy volume in terms of actual images, a thick one in terms of the emotions it conjures. The brevity of our meetings spawned unopened pages of possibilities. Was it the same for him? I wonder. What does he look like today? Is he still as handsome? If we were to walk past each other on the street, we probably wouldn't recognise one another. How could we? Decades have passed since I last saw him. Yet of all the people I have ever met, I am convinced that what drew me to Alexander in the first place—that magnetic essence of his—still lies there in its cocoon-like form, uncorrupted, buried beneath the layers of the life he has built for himself.

114

I wish I hadn't received that phone call. I am now thinking of Alexander again and it is getting in the way. I remember what Paola told me: that he was a promise cut short. For a while, every time my mobile phone rings I run. And every time it isn't him feels like tripping over a step. Like a promise cut short again.

115

Alexander Karlick

116

He calls when I'm in the shower, late for the school run. I see a foreign number on my phone as I'm dashing out the door with the girls. My hair is still wet, I have no makeup on, and I missed Alexander's call.

What is it? Katia asks, looking at me strangely as I board the bus in an agitated state. I can tell he's left me a message and all I want to do is listen to it. But I'm going to have to wait until the girls are out of sight.

I missed a call, I tell her. Someone I haven't seen in many years. But it's not important.

Is it a girl or a boy?

A girl, I answer after a brief moment of hesitation.

You're lying. Katia's eyes are glaring, like those of an angry adult.

Why are you saying that?

Because I know you're lying. I can feel it.

It's the truth, I reply, trying to conceal the tremor in my voice. I think you're just angry, which I understand. It's normal to be angry. And I know all these changes have been difficult for you and Lola, I add. But things will get better, I promise.

No they won't and nothing is normal, she says.

Hey, this is Alexander. I think you must remember me even though it's been it's been like, I don't know, twenty-five years? Anyway, I'm coming to London next week and I thought it'd be good to see you again. This is my number if you'd like to call me back. Hope you'll be around. Bye.

His voice is raspy. Nervous too. The way his intonation rose when he mentioned how many years it's been. How it would be good to see me again. The way he cleared his throat between *week* and *I thought it'd be good*. The softness of *Hey*. Of *if you'd like to call me back*. The expectation behind *hope you'll be around*.

And in fact I won't be around, because my sister is getting married the following week. The timing could not have been worse. I must ring him back and explain.

I listen to his message several times. I can tell that he never forgot me. That, just like I have, he has been waiting for this moment for many years. He knows perfectly well that it's been twenty-five. He is no longer a shadow of the past. I will see him again. Not this time, but another. I do not know what will happen when I do. It is too early to speculate. The main thing is that I have an option. And knowing that fills me with joy. I have his number, he has mine: we can reach each other if we want to. If he chooses to read my book, he will recognise himself. What he will make of it, I do not know. What matters is that he is now close to me again. That the spell has been broken.

I dial his number a few times but hang up before pressing the final digit. Something is stopping me. I do not want my memory of him to be shattered. I fear that, if I speak to him, it might be. And I cannot bear a new shattering. I can feel the cold weight of it, unbalancing me.

117

At my sister's wedding, young and old dance together, holding hands in a circle. My mother is wearing a long red dress and matching lipstick. She laughs, clutching my brother-in-law's hand as the circle widens and the music swells. My father joins in. He hops from leg to leg as an accordion plays a *Klezmer* melody and a woman starts singing in a mellifluous voice. Arms are raised, and all of us spontaneously join her in song. A rush of hope fills me. My pregnant sister is carefully hoisted in a chair above the crowd. She throws her head back in laughter, and we all dance around her, our bodies whirling, leaping, cries of joy piercing the night air like constellations.

118

To live is to occupy a sequence of moments. To pass through time and place.

Here I stand, passing through this moment in time, dancing with my family and friends under the starry sky of a Provençal night.

I do not know that soon after my sister's wedding my father will fall ill. That the doctors will do all they can to save him. That the last sounds he will hear before dying are my mother's voice and a blackbird singing outside his Parisian hospital window.

119

This story began thirty-five years ago. My daughters are grown up now. We rarely discuss the past, and when we do it is briefly. Sometimes we look at photographs together. There are no recordings of that time. No tapes, films, or videos of any of us. There are only fragmented bits of memory, shards of a shattered marriage—long buried but never forgotten.

120

I never saw Alexander again. I met someone else instead. The man I love. We live together in a different country. We grow bougainvillea and jasmine, orange and olive trees.

The leaves rustle and glow in the dappled sunshine.

ERIS

86–90 Paul Street
London EC2A 4NE

265 Riverside Drive
New York NY 10025

ISBN 978-1-9997981-4-7

eris.press

ALBA ARIKHA is a novelist, poet, and musician. Her books include *Where to Find Me* (longlisted for the 2020 Wingate Prize) and the acclaimed memoir *Major/Minor*.